Bolan gen
the deton

The sliding doc   like a
giant fist had slammed into it from inside the
building. One of the men who had been tugging at it
looked down in shuddering shock to where both of
his forearms lay on the ground, severed at the
elbows as the edge of the door shot by.

Then the secondaries went off. A ball of flame
came angrily billowing out of the space where the
door had been. No one had time to scream. The
cleansing fire turned them instantly into
smoldering cinders.

It was a deadly chain reaction. The next explosion
tore a ragged hole in the tin roof and a pillar of red
flame shot a hundred feet into the night sky.
Melting metal debris rained down onto the dusty,
rocky ground.

The hot breath of death blasted everything.

Other
MACK BOLAN
titles in the Gold Eagle
Executioner series

Mack Bolan's
ABLE TEAM

Mack Bolan's
PHOENIX FORCE

MACK BOLAN

THE EXECUTIONER 44

BOLAN

Terrorist Summit

DON PENDLETON

A GOLD EAGLE BOOK FROM

WORLDWIDE

TORONTO · NEW YORK · LOS ANGELES · LONDON

First edition August 1982

ISBN 0-373-61044-0

Special thanks and acknowledgment from the author
to Steven Krauzer for his contributions to this work.

Printed in Canada

What love does is to arm. It arms the worth
of life in spite of life.

—*Archibald MacLeish*

The root of the matter is a very simple and
old-fashioned thing . . . love or compassion.
If you feel this, you have a motive for existence,
a guide for action, a reason for courage,
an imperative necessity for intellectual honesty.

—*Bertrand Russell*

Love is a force. A force is a thing that moves
and does. Scratch the surface of a true warrior
and you will find inside a lover.

—*Mack Bolan,*
The Executioner

Dedicated to Barry Meeker (1942–1982), a soldier of fortune who rescued fleeing East Germans in three helicopter missions behind the Iron Curtain during the 1970s. A philosophy scholar who spoke six languages, Meeker was a daring and much-decorated helicopter pilot in the Vietnam war. He died in a helicopter crash near Hinton, Oklahoma. God bless.

<u>CLASSIFIED</u>: TOP <u>SECRET</u>
OPERATIONAL IMMEDIATE

FR WHITE HOUSE/BROGNOLA 231915Z
TO STONYMAN OPS/PHOENIX
BT
MISSION ALERT X EXERCISE FULL PREROGATIVES
X TOPMAN REQUESTS PHOENIX PERSONAL
HANDLING X DAUGHTER OF TOP US HI-TECH
CONTRACTOR HARRISON BRETON KIDNAPPED THIS
AM IN ALGIERS X DAYLIGHT STRIKE ON PUBLIC
STREET X BRETON'S FIRM DEVELOPING ULTRA
SECRET LOW YIELD NUCLEAR DEVICE CODENAMED
LITTLE BANG CAPABLE OF CONCEALMENT IN
STANDARD ATTACHE CASE X BRETON HIMSELF
DISAPPEARED SHORTLY AFTER NEWSBREAK X
LITTLE BANG PROTOTYPE ALSO MISSING X
IMPLICATIONS OBVIOUS X INTERCEPT BRETON
AND RECOVER PROTOTYPE AT ANY COST REPEAT AT
ANY COST X DATA PACKAGE IN COMPUTER FILE
ZEBRA X INCLUDES LOCATIONS KNOWN TERRORIST
SAFEHOUSES IN ALGIERS X EXERCISE OWN
DISCRETION RE KIDNAPPEE ONCE NATIONAL
SECURITY IMPERATIVES ACHIEVED X
ACKNOWLEDGE AND CONFIRM SOONEST
BT
231915Z
EOM

OPERATIONAL IMMEDIATE

FR STONYMAN 231942Z
TO BROGNOLA/WH/WASHDC
BT
PHOENIX SENDS RE LITTLE BANG X ACCEPT X
ENROUTE X FORWARD ALL DEVELOPING
PARTICULARS STONYMAN FOR RELAY ALGIERS
BT
231942Z
EOM

OPERATIONAL URGENT

FR STONYMAN 231955Z
TO BROGNOLA/WH/WASHDC
BT
APRIL SENDS RE LITTLE BANG X PHOENIX
LAUNCHED X ALL STONYMAN FORCES ALERTED FOR
STANDBY CONTINGENCIES X SUGGEST DESIGNATE
STONYMAN OPS MISSION CENTRAL FOR ALL COMM
DATA INTEL AND ALL OTHER MISSION
REQUIREMENTS X CLEAR COMSAT LINK ALL USEMB
IN TARGET REGION X CLEAR NAVCOMM LINK NSS
WASHDC COMSIXTHFLT FOR MISSION SUPPORT
REQUIREMENTS
BT
231955Z
EOM

Mack —

    Here's my digest of the material Aaron dug up on Harrison Breton, his daughter Jill, and Project Little Bang. Good luck — be careful.

        I love you

            April

Harrison Payne Breton, age 57, residence Palo
Alto, CA. Pres. & Chief Executive Officer,
Breton Indust. B.S., M.S. (M.I.T.); Fletcher
School of Diplomacy, Tufts University.

Subject served on National Security Council
1968-1979. Continues to serve as consultant
to Central Intelligence Agency.

Breton Industries is hi-tech electronics
firm specializing in design of advanced micro-
circuitry, esp. w/ ref. to weapons applications.
Major client is U.S. Department of Defense.

Subject is a widower.

Jill Marie Breton, age 22, last residence
Cambridge, MA. No employment. Attended Harvard,
dropped out junior year. Presently supported by
monthly stipend from father, Harrison Breton.

For the past 18 mos., subject has been
travelling in Europe & N. Africa. Arrived
Algiers 2 wks prior to this dossier.

Subject arrested once, charged with
disorderly conduct, fined $200.00. Charge
stemmed from role in anti-nuke rally at Seabrook,
NH. Subject has spoken at variety of
demonstrations, attracting media attention for
attacks on her father as "war profiteer," etc.

Psychological profile indicates subject's
anti-social attitudes not motivated by disloyalty
or subversive inclinations. Instead, subject
resents fact that her father has devoted so much
time to his business. Subject has publicly
stated: "I have no father."

<u>General description:</u> PROJECT LITTLE BANG

Project LB developed by Breton Industries under contract with DOD. LB involves the production of an extremely compact low-yield nuclear device designed to cause near-total destruction w/in a limited area; radius of primary impact is estimated to be 200 yards, plus or minus 10 yards. LB allows pinpoint targeting and insures to a degree greater than previously possible that noncombatant lives are spared. The technology exceeds current level of Soviet development by at least five development-years.

A prototype of LB has been manufactured. In size it is no bigger than a shoe box. It is under top /repeat top /security.

PROLOGUE

Mack Bolan had never thought of himself as some sort of savior. He had no grand illusions about himself or his role in life. He was a man, much like any other, not a superman, and he was limited by the same laws of physics and biology that govern the lives of all men. Bolan's difference was that he seldom sought the comfort zones. He could not dissociate his principles from his own conduct—that is, he could not believe in one world while living contentedly in another. There can be no doubt that this formidable warrior operated from a consistent and overriding world view which placed his own personal comfort at the bottom of priorities and it was a view which, the evidence shows, began forming in early childhood.

Some have said that Mack Bolan's chief difference lay in his considerable talents. And it is true, of course, that this man was the consummate warrior, a brilliant tactician and strategist, physically adept and mentally sharp, a weapons master. But talent does not, in and of itself, produce commitment. And Bolan's difference lay in his commitment. He did not seek personal comfort. He could take the heat and he could take the cold—as willing to run as to walk, to stand as to lie down, to labor as to rest. The deeper difference was that he cared—he always cared—and he cared about it all.

It has been suggested by various men of wisdom that "care" is synonomous with "love." To love someone is to care about that person's fate. It seems strange, then, that few people today associate fighting with loving. Indeed, a popular maxim of our time separates lovers from fighters. Yet the great rallying cry to warriors through the ages had concerned love of country, love of ideals, love of family and posterity.

Bloodlust does not move the true warrior. It did not move Mack Bolan. Love—*love*—moved Mack Bolan.

The world was a crass place, and the parts of it that Colonel John Phoenix was forced to inhabit were particularly unilluminated. But within the ignorant darkness shone a light, and it was visible wherever love flowed between people.

The love, for example, of a father for a daughter, the respect that ennobled with light the biological connections of life, the familial caring that Mack Bolan understood to the depths of his being.

It was this love that now propelled him to one of the pits of the world. He would need all the light he could get.

1

Mack Bolan palmed the doorknob and turned it slowly, silently, until he felt the latch retract. He pushed the door forward a fraction of an inch, then took a step back.

The flat of his right foot slammed into the door so hard that wood cracked as it burst open.

Bolan came in behind it, dropping to a half-crouch, sweeping the room with the muzzle of the Beretta Brigadier. A single hardman was sitting at a table opposite. He had a swarthy complexion with long stringy hair and a well-padded gut. He stared at the black apparition in front of him, the sandwich in his hand frozen halfway between the table and his gaping mouth.

The guy broke the pose and lunged for the auto-pistol next to his plate.

Before his hand could close on the weapon, a silenced 9mm Parabellum snorter snapped his head back. An ugly third eye appeared in the middle of his forehead. It began to leak fluids. The half-eaten sandwich flew away in a lazy arc from his hand and splattered against the wall.

Bolan stepped to the window and parted a curtain to check his backtrack. From the outside this hardsite appeared to be nothing more than a large and expensive home, the two-story modern structure not much different from its neighbors in this part of el-Biar, the fashionable suburb west of Algiers. It sat halfway up the slope of the Sahel Hills. Below it Bolan could see the high-rise buildings of the Algerian capital itself, the cement and marble gleaming white in the midday sun. Beyond was the Bay of Algiers and the endless blue of the Mediterranean.

Cars passed on the Rue Gaid Malika, the boulevard that wound across the end of the hardsite's sloping lawn. Most were expensive European compacts, with an occasional top-of-the-line sports car. None of the drivers or passengers paid any attention to the house.

The Executioner had visited Algeria once before. When that particular trip was over, the one-time empire of Don Cafu, Mafia monarch of Sicily's Agrigento province, lay in ruins. To an extent his victory then accounted for why Mack Bolan was back in Algeria now: his success rate at striking—alone finally—at the most major of leagues was impressing others other than his enemies, whom it impressed mightily. Today the White House, America One in the oval office, was fervently in support of him.

True, the world did not know of Colonel John Phoenix. No dignitaries recognized him on his now-extensive travels; no newspaper reporter knew enough to quiz him or track down his friends for a "quote." He was an unknown.

But for an unknown he enjoyed access to unusual byways. In the area of armament, he could count on instant acquisition of all the latest pieces, from caseless rifles to hand-carried missiles. Stony Man's new armorer was a wizard, but remote, serious: only the best for him, what really worked in the most serious of circumstances, nothing flashy. And Bolan bought that. It gave him confidence in his back-up, in that rare line-up of people who did know who he was, and what he had to do.

He had to be in Algeria because this inflammable, unpredictable North African desert nation was still the last refuge of the crazies and the criminals of an anomalous globe. Still the one filthy old used-up oil drum that hid every hothead that banged his head against the natural order elsewhere.

The door behind the dead sentry led into a large open hallway. An entrance to one side revealed a meeting room, with a conference table that could seat two dozen. It was empty. A row of doors lined the other side of the hall—smaller meeting rooms and a pantry. There was no further sign of life on this floor, but from the head of the wide stairway at the end of the hall came the indistinct murmur of two men talking, and the faint sound of music. The living quarters would be up there.

The man from blood was halfway up the wide staircase, his rubber-soled sneakers silent on the carpeted risers, when the Arab gunner at the top spotted him. The Arab was sitting in a straight-back chair tipped against the far wall, gazing at a magazine. There was a picture of two naked women and a man on the cover, with a caption in Arabic script, and the guard was holding the magazine open with both hands and turning it to various angles like he could see into the picture.

The leer on his face dissolved into bewilderment when he saw the stony figure in front of him. Then it turned into pop-eyed fear as he noted the extended Beretta. The Arab raised the skin mag as if it would protect him, but the steel-jacketed slug ripped through its glossy pages, decapitating the figure of one of the cavorting women. Then the book slipped from lifeless fingers and dropped to the Arab's lap. Blood from a pulsing throat wound splashed over its lurid photographs.

A door burst open at one end of the upstairs hall and two more of the (not so) safehouse's crew came charging out. One of them snarled obscenities in Arabic, but the second man said in English, "What the fuck...?"

The Beretta banged the air and snapped off the rest of the sentence. The top of a dirty-blond scalp lifted away and was hurled, wet, against the door. The guy's Arab buddy then got his ticket to Allah cored through his brains.

Bolan waited maybe ten beats, but nobody else emerged. Whoever was in the house was too preoccupied to pay attention to the ruckus in the hall. Bolan suspected the noise remained unheard; he smelled the faint odor of hashish smoke in the still air.

The room from which the two now-extinct hardmen had come was empty except for a small table and three folding chairs. On the table was a scattering of playing cards, a half-dozen empty beer bottles, an ashtray full of butts. One of the chairs had been knocked over.

A man was tied to it.

He was in his mid-fifties but looked fit. He had a full head of silvery hair and a tanned face that would have been handsome but for the livid shiner around his right eye and the ragged cut across his left cheek. There was blood on the front of his white linen shirt. His chin was slumped on his chest. As Bolan came in the captive managed to raise his head. There was fear in his eyes, and pain, and resignation.

"I told you," he said, in a tired, strained voice. "I'm ready to deal. Just for God's sake tell me what you want."

He saw Bolan resheath the silenced Beretta. "You're not one of them?"

"I'm a friend, Mr. Breton," Bolan said. "I don't have time for anything except some fast answers from you." He pulled the man and chair upright, then drew a thin-bladed Fairbairon-Sykes stiletto from his utility belt and went to work on Breton's bonds. "How long have you been here?"

Breton suddenly shuddered. His face went white with delayed shock. "Are they all. . . is it over?"

"Snap out of it," Bolan ordered sharply. He did not need the man to go to pieces now.

"I've been here only about an hour," Breton said. His hands were free. He buried his face in them in exhaustion.

"Where is the Little Bang prototype?"

"You know—?" Breton straightened.

"Please answer the question, Mr. Breton. Lives depend on it, including your daughter's."

"It's safe and secure." Breton dug a handkerchief from his pocket, hunched his shoulders and daubed at the cut on his cheek. "One of my subsidiary companies, Consolidated Petroleum Research Consultants, is based here in Algiers. The prototype is in its vault."

Breton looked up, as if appealing to the big man in black. "I never meant to give it to them—I thought perhaps they would take money. But the one in charge wouldn't even talk about it. He said it could wait, that he had more important things to do. I think he was on drugs. He left me with those other two, and they never said anything either. They just beat me every once in a while, for no reason at all. It meant no more to them than opening another bottle of beer."

"You were out of your league, mister," Bolan said. "Listen carefully. When I get you out of here, go directly to the American Embassy. They're expecting you, and they'll put you in contact with a man named Harold Brognola. Brognola will arrange to get you and the Little Bang prototype back to the States. You do nothing except what he tells you."

Breton nodded his understanding.

"Now stay here until I get back."

"Wait a moment, please." Breton pulled himself unsteadily to his feet. "You are aware that my daughter has been kidnapped?"

"Yes."

"You must understand. Jill and I were never close. I was caught up in my work, and I thought it was enough to give her things—money, clothes, travel, an education. She could have whatever she desired."

"Very loving," Bolan said.

"I know," Breton responded to the irony in his fellow American's tone. "I am possessed by my guilt—that's why I charged in here with no thought for the consequences."

"You risked your life for her, Mr. Breton," Bolan said. "That's more than some men would do."

"It's not enough. I want one more chance. One last chance to make it work with her. Promise me you will save my daughter."

Unbidden, the images of Bolan's own family, terrorized by Mafia butchers, came distressingly to mind, and the nightfighter felt a sudden kinship for the man standing before him.

Bolan took Breton's hand in a firm grasp.

"You got it," he said.

"Thank you," the older man replied. "I know you will succeed."

But what if the girl was already dead?

Bolan turned and left the room. His briefing had given him a very good idea where he could find the answer.

2

The Executioner had only just returned from Vietnam, a victor once more. With Jack Grimaldi's invaluable help, Bolan had struck fast and deep—and had made sure with the blood of evil men that he would pay only the price of a nicked ear for the salvation of hapless American victims in that ultimate kill zone in the Far East. Paid in flesh, that is. In spirit it was a wrenching psychic experience that agonized him like all his other miles.

Now he was out on a limb again, and more alone than ever. Bolan knew this one would be a solo hellground, he could feel it in his gut. Hell, he could feel it in the scab on his earlobe. He could feel it from deep in the sore bones through to the weathered exterior of the over-extended warrior.

The more he succeeded, prevailed, the more America needed him. That was the way of history. And also true was that with each blow, each strike, the growing population of his back-up system made him more alone than ever.

Here in this land of sand and rock he would have no consoling conversations with April Rose, no osmotic understanding with Hal Brognola that could cut communication time in half. No fraternal assistance from Able Team. No comradeship with the brave newcomers of Stony Man's Phoenix Force, fresh from a bloodying in Argentina just prior to that country's dust-up with the Old World.

No, now Bolan himself was in the old world and it was a world a million miles from his people. He was howlingly, achingly alone.

That, again, was the way of history, and that's the way his country wanted it. His government needed him because he and he alone could strike the fear of the unknown into those who had gotten democracy over a barrel.

He could do it because he *was* the unknown.

Algeria stank. It smelled of the burnt-nerve frustration of nuclear stand-off. It smelled of the future, of ashes. Radioactive threats grew floridly in this hot arid wasteland. The politics of Algeria allowed the very basest elements of a disintegrating scene to reside and flourish here, to prosper in the cancerous manner of death-in-life.

Again, that is why Bolan was chosen. Algeria was asking for trouble. And it was going to get it. From the unknown.

The biggest mistake here in the Third World was its typically reckless acceptance, indeed encouragement, of the new union between terrorism and organized crime. Far in time and space from this lifeless North African land, the tentacles had begun to wrap around the world of organized crime seeking a new vehicle, a new method, for its poisonous seizures of power.

Those tentacles gripped the entire continental United States; they stretched to Hawaii in the west, London and France and Sicily to the east, the Caribbean to the south, Montreal to the north.

In fact it was in Montreal that the ruling cartel of crime first attempted to organize a *Cosa di Tutti Cosi*, a Thing of All Things, on an international scale. Delegates from all over the U.S. as well as from Switzerland, Germany, France, Japan and South America used the cover of the Olympic Games to consolidate on an international scale.

Some timely intercession from a certain man in black extinguished the plan, but not the underlying notion. As soon as the Executioner turned his unfathomable talents against the shakers and movers of worldwide terrorism, he became aware that his old antagonists were very much a part of the terrorist infrastructure.

The Stony Man computer had outputted hard data that proved the Mafia-terrorist link.

Fact: The Organization—the underground confederation of the Red Brigades, the Front Line, and hundreds of lesser known terrorist cells—regularly hired Mafia hitmen to murder potentially hostile witnesses.

Fact: The Mafia's Calabria branch, known as 'Ndrangheta, had become almost a silent partner of the Organization, helping to rob banks, steal artworks, kidnap, kill—for a one-half share of the take.

When the Red Brigades snatched shipbuilder Angelo Costa in an operation that would serve to finance the later abduction and eventual murder of Aldo Moro, the $2.5-million ransom was split 50/50 with the 'Ndrangheta Matthews.

As one of Stony Man Farm's authorities on global terrorism had advised Bolan in a chilling briefing: *"Half the take goes to an organization with lofty revolutionary pretensions, robbing in order to kill. The other half goes to common crooks who habitually kill in order to rob."*

This was Bolan's new knowledge, the constantly extending foundation of his philosophy: Whatever terrorists call themselves—"people's liberation soldiers," "freedom fighters"—their purpose is, like that of the Mafia, to profit from someone else's loss while cloaked in the facelessness and buoyed by the pressurized might of *the group*.

This understanding, divined during his sojourns in the lush Virginia hill country, was the Executioner's way of facing and focusing his gut feelings and converting them to become an asset to the total man.

Now he was in the sick terrain of urban Algeria, and thought was replaced by action.

From the room at the other end of the hall a woman giggled. The sound was unnatural and forced, and had nothing to do with happiness or pleasure. Bolan moved silently toward it. The Beretta belched a pencil of flame and the latch of the closed door before him shattered. Bolan gave it his foot and proceeded into the room. Hal had fingered this as the place.

It looked like a bizarre fantasy out of *One Thousand and One Arabian Nights*. The windowless walls were loosely draped with red gauze, backlit by strangely shaped lamps with spouts and handles. More gauze hung in folds from the ceiling. The radio, an old-fashioned tube model, sat in the corner, the sounds of Arab deejay prattle dribbling out of it in futility. The only piece of furniture was a low table on which sat an oversized hookah water-pipe with intricate coils of blown glass. The air was fetid with the sticky-sweet perfume of hashish.

Most of the floor was covered with plush red cushions and pillows. A nude woman lay back against the far wall in a pile of them. She was dark-skinned and very pretty, her delicate facial features contrasting with the ripe swell of her breasts and hips. Her wrists were tied together, the rope looped through a ringbolt set in the wall over her head. Her legs were awkwardly splayed.

The white man standing over her was also naked, except for a pair of cowboy boots and a Stetson hat. He was very slim, his skin pale, his dark hair unkempt and hanging down to his shoulders.

The girl took one look at the blacksuit in the doorway and the giggle came to a choking end. Her eyes turned up in their sockets and she passed into a dead faint.

The naked guy blinked, like he was hoping this

dude with the big gun was some kind of bad trip brought on by the hash.

Bolan pulled the Fairbairon stiletto from its sheath on his belt. The naked guy put up one hand, took a step back, said, "Hey, man..."

"Stow it," Bolan ordered. The girl's chest was rising and falling with regular steady breathing. Bolan leaned over and slashed through the rope she was hanging from in one cut. She flopped limply into the cushions. The naked guy watched all of this through wide eyes. He wished he had his pants on.

Bolan pressed the muzzle of the Beretta against the guy's forehead, just above the bridge of his nose. The guy stumbled backward, stopped when he came to the wall. Bolan pressed the gun against his pale skin.

"Where's the girl, Tex?" Bolan said in a deadly voice.

"What girl?"

Bolan thumbed back the hammer of the Brigadier. In his lifetime—sometimes it seemed like several lifetimes—the man known as the Executioner had become really quite good at the art of interrogation. A naked man feels particularly defenseless. Especially when a warm gun barrel is drilling a hole in his skull. What was important now was to make the fear of death the pinpoint focus of all consciousness, because Bolan had to cut through this punk's hashish fog. The numbers left no time to wait for the doper to get straight.

"Where's the girl, Tex?" Bolan said again.

The guy seemed to actually, physically shrink.

"Look, man," Tex said, "I had nothing to do with her. Listen, I even told Harker to leave her be, I swear to God. I never touched her, man. You can't tie me in to that one."

"Yeah," Bolan told the guy. "I can."

"Harker doesn't listen anymore," Tex said. His mind was unhinged with fear. "He doesn't listen to me, doesn't listen to anyone. Doesn't tell me anything either, just leaves me back here to play with myself."

Bolan knew he was about to lose the guy. He tapped him across the face three times with the barrel.

"You do know where the girl is, Tex," he said. Now he sounded almost gentle.

Very slowly, the doped-up terrorist nodded yes.

"This is all very simple," Bolan said carefully. He pulled back the automatic, let Tex see it a foot in front of his face.

"I want you to tell me where she is. If you don't I'm going to kill you. One shot through the skull."

In the opposite corner the Arab girl moaned and drew a brown arm across her breasts.

Something snapped in Tex. When he sat and began to talk it was in a steady monotone. Bolan knew this about opiate users. One minute they'd be in dreamland, the next they'd crash to earth like sacks of wet cement.

"You gotta understand about Algeria," Tex said

slowly. "First time Harker and I came here was just after we had to leave the States fast. We needed someplace where we wouldn't be hassled. Algeria welcomes, uh, you know, certain types. We've seen the German Red Army Faction here, the Italian Red Brigades, the IRA, the Basques, the PLO. The Algerians have been like this since their revolution against the French in '62. They did the same for Harker and me that they did for Eldridge Cleaver back in 1969. And we did certain favors in return."

"What kind of favors?"

"You know, jobs. They sort of sent Harker out with other groups—Palestinians, mostly. Kidnapping, hijacking, bombing."

Bolan's face went hard with anger. The other man realized he had rambled on too much.

"Hey man," Tex said quickly. "I'm talking about Harker, talking straight like you said. That's not me, that violence shit isn't my bag. I'm chickenshit, man."

"Yeah," Bolan said. "And your time is running down."

"The girl, right," Tex said quickly. He wet his lips with the tip of his tongue. The dope seemed to be wearing off. "Okay. Harker's got a compound, a basecamp, in the Tanezrouft, which is right in the middle of the goddamn Sahara, maybe 800 miles south of here. It's still in Algeria, but it's only about 50 miles north of the Mali frontier. That's where he took the girl."

Tex stared at the big man in black. Now that his head was clearing, he understood as he looked at his adversary exactly how close he came to having his brains blown all over these fancy gauze-draped walls. His eyes had become pools of animal fear.

"Truth, man," he whispered, his gaze riveted on the probing gun. "I swear it."

"Is she alive?"

"Yes," Tex bleated. "Honest to God, man, she's good as new."

"Convince me."

"I talked to Dick Wolfe on the radio just before the girl's old man showed up here. Wolfe, that's Harker's right-hand man, he says—he *said* . . ."

Bolan twitched the barrel of the Beretta to remind the half-stoned terrorist to get on with it.

"He says Harker is still having a good time with the Breton chick. Messing with her, you know? He likes them young. He won't off her until he has to. That's tomorrow noon at the earliest—that was the deadline he gave Breton."

"And Harker doesn't know Breton is here?"

"He don't know nothing about that, man. I was going to radio him when the old man showed, but, like, I got stoned, there was the chick—" he nodded at the Arab girl disabled with dope "—so I figured it could wait."

"Figuring like that saved your life, guy," Bolan told him. "It gave me a reason to keep you breathing."

Tex stared into the Beretta's inner depths.

"Get dressed," Bolan ordered.

"Huh?"

"You're taking me to that compound."

"No way. Nobody, not even the Algerian government— Listen, man, if I do that, Harker will kill me."

"And if you don't—"

"Don't say it, man." Tex drew his skinny frame erect and moved past Bolan. "I'll get my duds."

"You do that," Bolan said with the cold precision of a sculptor's chisel.

3

Mack Bolan's Third Mile was not a fight he had asked for. It was a fight that had sought him out, a menace that so clearly demanded his warrior skills that the man, that other man called the Executioner, could not help but respond—even if it meant returning from the dead, from the ashes of his last killing mile, to arise as John Phoenix: new features, same fierce captaincy over the forces of slaughter.

He did not inquire what one man alone could do.

He did what had to be done.

It was not vengeance that motivated Mack Bolan to wage his one-man offensive against the Cosa Nostra. The nightfighter always knew that the death of ten thousand vermin could not recreate the life of one good man or woman. It was more an instinct that made him do it, an innate sense of right that told the blitzkrieg guy that the very existence of the many-tentacled Mafia octopus tainted the life of every American. He could not but respond. He hacked off those tentacles and chopped them into offal.

His hit-and-git attacks had become a trademark. This consummate warrior understood psychological warfare better than most psychologists. And then he had learned to infiltrate the Mafia's deepest reaches, refining the art of ''role camouflage'' to such a degree that he could pass himself at will as a member of the Syndicate's Ace corps.

So yeah, it was not hard to see how there came a point when the name of Mack the Bastard was enough to send the *capos* into the undignified, looking-over-the-shoulder paranoia of the scared shitless. Their psycho dance of fear was right on: he was out to get them, and get them he did.

The skills that he acquired could be learned by others, perhaps as well as by Mack Bolan. But the qualities that made him the only man who could undertake this New War against international terrorism could not be learned. They came from within the man himself.

He lived and breathed off the fumes of America's rage: his blood pulsed with the very life of blood spilled by civilization's ruthless enemies. His senses were never more vigorous than when assaulted by the putrefaction of his foe.

The Executioner had no deep-seated need to fight, no need for any frequent and bloody release of aggression. His strongest feeling was of sadness. It was his guide in this stinking world, his yardstick for what was most true, most relevant, most urgent.

He felt sadness that the new war was necessary. Sadness at the pervasiveness of terror, repression, and violence. Profound sadness at the international scope and enormity of the threat that mad men posed.

Men who destroyed for the sake of ideology.

Men who killed solely for the taste of blood.

Men like Luke Harker, who in his megalomania believed he had a date with destiny.

But Harker—like others before him—was going to learn his true fate.

Luke Harker's date was with the Executioner.

A brilliant canopy of stars threw a light over the desert that was so bright the headlights of the Land Rover were unnecessary. Ahead of them Bolan could see ghostly expanses of open rock desert.

Tex Hoffman was driving the old roofless British 4WD vehicle, staring straight ahead through the windshield, the fingers of his right hand drumming nervously on the steering wheel. Occasionally he tugged at the brim of his Stetson. Bolan, who had been briefed on this man's name and number by Stony Man printout, figured Tex got his name from his bent for cowboy-style clothes. He also reckoned that his fetish for all things Western was Hoffman's subconscious effort to deny his past and establish a new image. In fact Hoffman was the youngest son of a Manhattan executive and had never been west of Philadelphia until he was twenty.

"Don't you ever sleep?" Tex said, breaking the night silence. No answer. "You don't have to worry about me jumping you," he went on.

"Thanks," Bolan said at last.

"Lemme tell you something, man—you scare the living hell out of me."

Bolan leaned forward in the Rover's stiff-sprung seat and lit a cigarette, cupping his hands to avoid the slipstream. At midnight the temperature was in the mid-forties, the air almost refreshing as the powerful but rattling old rig sped through the night. This was as cool as it got in the North African desert.

"I'll tell you something else," Tex went on. "You can believe me or not, but it's the truth. All this violence business, the killings, the assassinations, that all scares the hell out of me too. Luke Harker, he thrives on that stuff. He doesn't *have* to do the dirty work himself anymore, but he does it all the same. He likes it, man. It gives me the creeps."

"Tell me about Luke Harker," Bolan said.

Tex Hoffman let out a deep breath. "Harker was in college when the Vietnam protest broke out in 1968, '69, but he was a couple of years older than the rest of us, and a jailbird already, long before the political arrests. In the summer of '69 he went to Cuba with the Venceremos Brigades, can you believe that?" The green Rover bounced along over the endless terrain.

Yeah, Mack Bolan could believe it, for sure. Under the guise of a program for assisting the agricultural poor in Cuba, the Venceremos episode had been one of the first direct attempts by Russia to recruit Americans into the armies of international terrorism.

In 1968, the Soviet Union had forced Castro into a secret agreement. In it, the Cuban dictator surrendered control of both his foreign policy and his security agency—the Dirección General de Inteligencia—to the Kremlin. Immediately, Colonel Viktor Simenov of the Soviet KGB was given an office adjoining that of the DGI head, and it was Simenov who directed the agency from that point on.

One of his first projects was the Venceremos Brigade. Twenty-five hundred young Americans came to Cuba, supposedly to cut sugarcane. Most of them did, but a few were selected by Simenov—recruited, trained, and returned to the U.S. to sow social disorder wherever they could.

Luke Harker, already a criminal, a misfit, a dangerous and unpredictable man, was a star pupil in that place.

"Harker had charisma," Tex Hoffman claimed. "He knew how to get people to like him and to do what he wanted. He had this hypnotic power over the crowd."

"Others had it before him," Bolan observed quietly. "Hitler. Manson."

Tex continued. He told his brooding passenger about how he and Richard Wolfe had joined up with the weird, erratic, ill-tempered Harker in time for the bloody Chicago riots of the Democrats' Convention.

Wolfe became the brains of Harker's blood-lust outfit, but he stayed behind the scenes at all times. He did not have Harker's magnetism, but Wolfe was the one who could control Harker when the psycho in him got out of hand.

At Chicago, Luke Harker and Richard Wolfe had jumped a young rookie cop. Wolfe held him down while Harker tore off the man's helmet and beat his brains in with his own riot stick. It was Wolfe's one big mistake, to involve himself so uncharacteristically and so deliberately in Harker's impulsive tantrum. It was the first serious slip in a slide to hell for them both. Hell was here, North Africa, right now. May that young rookie rest in peace.

Harker and Wolfe were charged with murder, but they disappeared before they could be arrested. The two of them surfaced in Santa Barbara, California, reunited with Tex Hoffman. There they took credit for the bombing of a suburban bank branch in which a dozen people were injured, five of them maimed for life. Maimed means limbs missing.

"I wasn't within 200 miles of Santa Barbara," Tex insisted, "but I confessed to underground press sources that I'd been in on the robbery, because I wanted in on the glory. That's how it was back then, you know?"

"Go on," Bolan ordered.

"Well, we came here, didn't we? With the contacts Harker had made through the Venceremos gig, we got along pretty well straight off. The Palestinians were just setting up their European network, and Carlos Ramirez—the one called the Jackal—was in charge of their 'European Directorate' in Paris, and he was recruiting. So we got work. A lot of work. More work than ever.

"I didn't have the stomach for it and they knew it. Not that kind of work. I'm too squeamish. I guess the main reason they kept me around was to keep an eye on me, make sure I wasn't gonna blow the whistle. They never did trust me."

"Neither do I, guy," said Bolan.

Tex glanced at the big American with what he hoped was a dirty look but which came out as an expression of spoiled annoyance. As a bodycock, Tex was a joke. A sick joke. "So Harker got some money together, and Wolfe made the right friends, and they started their own gang and used it to get more money. Now he's got this bunch he calls the Third World People's Liberation Front. It's really a private terrorist army that he'll rent to anyone who can pay the freight."

After twenty or so miles of driving across the cool, flat expanse of desert, the two men saw the moon peer over the horizon, big and pale and green.

"Man," Tex said wearily, "I never wanted to tear apart the United States. When I started with that crazyman Harker, I thought I was doing the best thing for my country. Protesting the war and everything, right? Then it got out of hand, and then I took part credit for the Santa Barbara bombing..." He shook his head at the lunacy of his past decisions. "So in the States they've got me for murder. And that's nothing compared to what Harker will do to me if I ever try to split on him."

"You got no deal, Hoffman," Bolan said harshly. "Get this straight—I don't like you. You're a thief, an extortionist, and you've spent the better part of your life stepping on people who weren't strong enough to stop you."

Bolan felt the anticipation of a killing ground soon to come, the fires of retribution soon to blaze in this desert that surrounded them here, a place too hot in the day for his blacksuit and too cool at night for anything but the chill hatching of plans for explosions now long overdue. "You're going to do what I say when I say it," he told Tex Hoffman. "The only thing you get in return is the fact that while you're with me you're safe from Luke Harker."

"But am I safe with you?" Tex smiled spinelessly.

"You keep asking yourself that, guy."

Bolan got a map from the jockey-box, folded it to the relevant sector of the Algerian Sahara Desert. They were about two hundred miles out from their objective, about four hours at the pace they were making.

Bolan had heard enough about Harker.

The tinpot terrorist was by far the worst pig among the array of people he himself had called pig in his anti-capitalist campaigns. To call Harker pig was to malign a fine animal.

Bolan knew Harker's type. As the moonlit desert sped by, he reflected on Man's penchant for money in the bank at whatever cost. That's what had gotten Harker by the balls, that had perverted his drive for glory. Greed was gripping the sick guy in his vitals. But Bolan spared no further thought on Harker.

He knew how it was that men went wrong, and crazy men went from wrong to wrong, bailing themselves out of desperate, hurtful psychodramas by stealing money, then killing for money. He knew that. And he knew how it would end.

It would end in hellfire.

Hellfire here on earth.

Fire in the midst of this hellish desert—and hundreds and hundreds of miles away from wherever money made sense or had any power.

About the blaze to come, Bolan spent a great deal of thought, in silence, in the deepest hours of night.

4

Immense *areg*, chains of undulating sand dunes, stretched off into the starlit distance. *Hamada*, rocky plateaus, jutted out of the sand dune basins. The Land Rover passed through a region of sandstone platforms that were called *tassili*, cut by the long-dry gorges of ancient rivers.

There was variety, sure. But it was of the most desolate kind. They had passed the last village several hours back, a small oasis *mechta* called Reggane.

At the height of summer, it could reach 120 degrees by the afternoon. Bolan had been informed that in this country, years could pass between rainfalls. It was complete barrenness.

They entered the region known as the Tanezrouft just before dawn. This was the bleakest landscape in the world, with the exception of the Poles. It was a vast pebble-covered plain that stretched to the western horizon, completely devoid of water, vegetation, or any form of sustenance that could support life. Nothing stirred. The only colors were shades of brown and gray.

After endless hours of driving through the Country

of the Dead, the Rover was now parked behind an outcropping of sand-blasted rock that formed part of a larger bluff. Below and about four hundred meters away was Luke Harker's terrorist base.

In this predawn hour it was necessary in Bolan's preliminary recon of the compound to make sightings through infrared nightsight binoculars: their seven-power magnification brought the details of the hardsite into sharp and detailed relief. Harker's camp was laid out in a square roughly two hundred meters to a side, surrounded by chain-link fencing topped with razor-wire. Platform towers—each with an oversized swivel-mounted searchlight—commanded the corners. In the midst of the awesome monotony of the desert, it was an extraordinary sight.

The single gate was in the middle of the side that Bolan faced. It was flanked by a guard station. As Bolan focused the binoculars on the entrance, an open jeep carrying two men pulled up from inside the camp. Early risers. A guard came out of the guardhouse, spoke briefly to the driver, then opened the gate and let the vehicle out. It veered around the compound, away from Bolan's position. A security patrol. Bolan checked the luminous dial of his watch and made a mental note.

The largest structures in the compound were four quonset huts grouped to one side. One had oversized doors cut into its near end, and Bolan made it as the garage. Another would be an armory, the others likely were billets. High-voltage wires radiated from a smaller building in the same area, which meant it housed a generator.

The field glasses brought a man into sharp relief, and immediately Bolan knew he had hit the bull's-eye. Straight to the heart of things. Luke Harker had changed his image from what was portrayed in the dossier photos that Bolan had studied in his briefing from Stony Man. But there was no mistaking his identity. It was Harker striding off into the darkness. He was in his early forties and had taken some sort of care of himself over the years. He stood straight, erect, his tall wiry frame clothed in blousy khakis and high laced boots. There was none of the hippie-style war protester about him. His dark hair seemed cropped short at the sides and he wore a billed cap. Smart. And uptight. Beneath the cap his features were angular; his bony face was composed of a series of hard-edged geometric figures. High cheekbones and small dark eyes were bisected by the V of his eyebrows, and his mouth was set in a hard line as he moved into an inspection of his domain before sun-up.

Bolan was stowing the powerful glasses in their case when he heard the whine of a vehicle's engine. It was growing louder.

Several flight bags nestled under one of the fold-down seats in the rear of the Rover. From one of these Bolan removed an M-203 autorifle, placed it to one side, and took out an Ingram M-10 machine pistol. He attached the wire stock to the butt, then threaded the suppressor to the muzzle. Sound carried alarmingly well in the airless desert atmosphere.

"Get in the rig," Bolan ordered Tex as he jammed a 30-round magazine into the machine pistol's grip. "Driver's seat."

"Wait a minute."

"Get in the rig," the big man repeated.

The jeep came over a low rise fifty feet ahead, just as Tex Hoffman settled behind the Rover's wheel.

The driver was hardly more than a kid. The man riding shotgun was Oriental. He was hugging an AK-47 and as the jeep lurched to an abrupt halt he began to clamber out to get firing room.

The driver stood up. "What you doing there?" he called out in English. But his partner was not about to wait for an answer.

The Oriental was out of the rig and leveling the Kalashnikov on Tex when a barely visible black-clad warrior stepped out from behind the Rover. The guard hesitated for a split second in the gray light, and the time stretched into an eternity. A controlled burst of eight 9mm flesh shredders spewed out of Bolan's Ingram and quietly stitched the guy from crotch to throat.

The driver shrieked in shock and sank back into his seat, his foot planted on the accelerator. But he had neglected to put the jeep in gear and the engine roared ineffectually. It was the last error in a brief and mistake-filled life.

The Ingram spoke again and the freestanding windshield shattered into nothingness a microsecond before the angry swarm of slugs tore most of the guy's head off his shoulders.

For a moment, nothing but silence filled the desert. Then Tex Hoffman's soft whisper: "Jesus Christ." He lowered his forehead to the steering wheel. "Jesus Goddamn Christ."

Bolan did not look back at him as he advanced toward the jeep. Suddenly there was something very pathetic about this terrorist named Allen "Tex" Hoffman.

Sure.

The guy had just found out what terror really meant.

5

Richard Wolfe looked down at the transcription of the radio message and read it over again, his lips pursed in a sour expression. Mornings were not his favorite time of the day—especially mornings on which he was rousted out of bed before dawn and told there was real trouble.

He vented some of his annoyance on the radio operator. "You make goddamn sure this stays under your hat," he snapped.

"I already forgot it," the operator said sullenly.

"Make sure it stays that way."

It was going to be a long damn day. Outside the air-conditioned atmosphere of the radio shack, the dry desert air pressed down on Wolfe like the hand of God, although it was still relatively cool. If you could call 80 degrees cool. Wolfe felt the sweat dampen his clothing. Great drops of it made greasy smears across his eyeglasses. He didn't bother to wipe them, it was too much effort. Wolfe had never been able to get used to this constant heat. Maybe it was the twenty extra pounds of gut he carried.

One of Harker's soldiers approached, his Kalashnikov AK-47 slung over a shoulder on a web belt. He gave Wolfe a halfhearted salute. Wolfe barely nodded in return. Harker was big on military discipline, but as far as Wolfe was concerned the demands for discipline were just another Harker power trip. He even had ranks. Harker was field marshal, because he liked the sound of the British title better than "general." Wolfe, to his own distaste, was major, and the rest of the TWPLF—the Third World People's Liberation Front—were divided into squads. All told, there were about 50 of Harker's men on base.

The private army had proven useful and profitable, Wolfe had to admit that. But there was a time when he had argued vigorously against building the compound. The location was absurdly isolated, the expense huge. Harker insisted that they had to start thinking big, and he accused Wolfe of being narrow-minded and shortsighted.

Crazy. Without Wolfe, Harker would still be trashing ROTC buildings in New Haven or holding love-ins at Golden Gate Park. It was Wolfe who wrote those clever speeches that got Harker an entire page of coverage in *Newsweek*. It was Wolfe who had dealt with the other terrorist contacts they had made in Europe and the Middle East, and Wolfe who had screened the terrorist assignments that they were offered, rejecting the ones that were unprofitable or too risky.

Goddammit. The desert heat was firing Wolfe's temper. I saved the guy's life twice and he probably doesn't even know it. Both times Harker was being maneuvered into a double-cross and both times Wolfe sniffed out the ambush and got them into safe territory before the heavy shit could come down.

The exasperated terrorist pushed into the hut that Harker called his Command Headquarters. He found himself sighing with gratitude as the first blast of air-conditioned coolness washed over him.

"You ever learn to knock, son?" Luke Harker said. He was grinning, but there was a hard edge to his tone, like he was making it clear just whose territory this was. He sat behind an old wooden desk, its edges scarred with scratches and cigarette burns.

The girl stood behind him, leaning over so her full breasts, barely contained by her neckerchief halter-top, rested on Harker's shoulders. Her hands were draped casually into his lap. She looked at Wolfe and took her time about letting Harker go. Below the halter she wore a pair of tight white shorts that rode below her navel. She was barefoot. Her toenails were painted pink.

They looked like they had been up all night.

Dammit, she knew how to get to a guy. Wolfe felt a thickening in his groin as he stared at her. Harker was leering at him; the son of a bitch got a real kick out of this. There was something about the guy that made women flop over and start panting, and Harker liked to flaunt it.

"To what do we owe the honor of your presence?" Harker was enjoying himself.

"We have to talk." Wolfe cocked his head significantly in the girl's direction.

"Why don't you go in the back, sugar, and straighten up a little," Harker said, still watching Wolfe.

"You can talk in front of me," the girl pouted. "Luke, you know I'm with you in whatever—"

"Jill." His tone brought the girl up short. "Don't make me say it again."

Momentary uncertainty crossed her features. Then she leaned down and nuzzled Harker's head, flashed a smile at Wolfe, and went through the door behind Harker's desk, swinging her hips for Wolfe's benefit.

Go ahead and shake your ass, baby, Wolfe thought viciously. 'Cause if I know Harker you won't be shaking anything pretty soon.

"Like the merchandise, Dick?" Harker said. "It's A-one prime goods."

Wolfe bit his lip and said nothing.

"You come around some time," Harker went on. "Maybe I'll let you watch."

At that moment, Richard Wolfe did not want to be the bearer of the bad news. Harker's mood had become so changeable. There was an ominous and increasing tendency to burst into rages. It had reached the point where even Wolfe was having trouble controlling him.

He took a breath and said: "We got trouble."

Harker's smirk continued undisturbed. "Yeah?"

"Someone hit the el-Biar hardsite," Wolfe said. "Hit it hard. Frank got back from Tripoli and went over to check it out. He says it looked like a fucking butcher shop. The doorman's brains were all over the wall. The three guys upstairs looked like they'd run into a meat grinder. Frank says there was a stream of dried blood halfway down the stairs.''

Harker stared glassily at him like a dead man and said: "Who?"

Wolfe shook his head, negative. "Frank found some Arab girl in Tex's room, half doped up, praying to Allah, scared out of her wits. All she saw was one guy—a big bastard, she says, tall, guns hanging off him, dressed in black."

"One guy, huh?" Harker snapped. "Get me Tex on the shortwave."

"That's the rest of it," Wolfe said. "Tex has disappeared."

Harker's palm slammed down on the desk. His face was tinged red. Wolfe took an involuntary step backward. The redness in the face, that was the first sign that Harker was going to blow up, and the blow-ups weren't always rational these days.

"That sellout son of a bitch," Harker snarled.

"Who?" Wolfe said, genuinely puzzled.

"Who the fuck do you think? Hoffman. The scrawny little bastard's hooked up with some other clown. This guy in black sounds like the right kind— hired muscle. Hoffman doesn't have the guts to pull something like this on his own. He knows what would happen—what's *gonna* happen to him."

"Why would Tex want to knock over the Algiers

safehouse?'' Wolfe made his tone as conciliatory as possible. "What's in it for him?"

"Taking over the territory. Making me look bad. How the hell do I know?"

"Listen," Wolfe said. "Don't worry about Tex. He's okay. There's not much trouble one guy can cause us. Even hired trouble. Right now we've got bigger fish to fry. Most of the delegations are already on base, and the rest will be in before the meeting tonight. Plus fifty of our boys are here to ride herd on them."

Harker nodded. He was regaining his equilibrium.

"Now," Wolfe went on. "What about the girl?"

Harker took a deep breath. "I want that goddamn bomb of her daddy's. It'll give us a card that will trump every one in their deck, and it's gonna make us king of the hill. With that little package, all the big boys are gonna bend down and kiss our rosy-red asses."

Harker grinned at his second-in-command. "You get back to Frank, you tell him to let me know the minute that package arrives in Algiers. If he doesn't take safe delivery by noon, we ice the chick."

"And if he does?"

Harker clasped both hands behind his neck and stretched comfortably. "We ice her anyway," he said.

Then he got up to patrol his domain before daylight.

6

It took him less than two minutes to breach the chain-link fence, using a small but effective pair of cutters from his belt.

Once inside, Bolan straightened up, checked his backtrack with a quick but all-seeing glance, then stalked onward into the nameless terrorist hellground.

In some ways it was the same battlefield on which all Man's many wars were fought.

The same one, yeah. And therefore not the last.

It was typical of the giant to go in like this, forever cocked and ready, poised at the edge of the howling plains of death, but calm, and quiet. Unless the numbers were falling too fast to leave time for caution, Mack Bolan never entered an arena without amassing all possible knowledge of it. There was no such thing as knowing too much, not in this kind of life. Not in this kind of death.

It was believing you knew too much that got guys killed.

During the Mafia campaigns there were those who said the guy had a death wish. Nothing could have been further from the truth. Mack Bolan had a highly developed *life* wish. And it wasn't the kind of wish that came true by charging in half-cocked.

There was no guard on the motor-pool garage. Bolan moved around the corrugated-metal building, stopping at several intervals to plant an explosive charge and install a remote radio-activated detonator. A sound investment in the future.

The directional antenna on top of one of the quonset huts was wired to a smaller building behind the armory—the radio shack. In this wilderness it would be the compound's only link with the outside.

The radio operator was visible, slumped back in his chair, his feet propped up on the table, dozing lightly. The receiver crackled softly with predawn atmospherics and snatches of disjointed voices. The noise didn't seem to be interfering with the guy's sleep.

But the pistol barrel did. As it jabbed into the back of the radio operator's neck, and a hand clamped hard over his mouth, the guy awoke in a hurry.

"I've got questions," Bolan whispered, "and I want quiet answers. You understand?"

The guy nodded yes against the pressure of Bolan's hand.

"The girl."

"She's here," the hardman gasped through the iron hand that held his face.

"Alive."

"Sure." The guy squirmed to find a more comfortable position. Bolan poked him hard with the Beretta and said, "Don't." The guy froze again. "Have you seen her?" Bolan demanded.

"Yes," the radioman grunted. "Everyone has. Harker lets her walk around the goddamn compound half-naked."

"You get to go on living, radioman," Bolan said near the guy's ear. "But only for as long as you tell it right. You were hit from behind—that's all you remember."

"Sure," the guy said quickly. "I was hit from..." The pistol barrel slammed into the base of his skull and returned him to dreamland. Bolan was not going to kill a defenseless man who had given what he was asked for. There was still time for mercy.

The shortwave transceiver was the latest solid-state model. Bolan removed the backboard to reveal the printed circuit boards lined up in a neat row. He removed four of them and secured them in a pocket. It was unlikely they would get replacement parts in that neighborhood.

He finished the job with the silenced Brigadier automatic, putting three slugs into the front of the radio. Its face shattered vividly. That was an insurance measure, but it was a psychological ploy as well.

The Executioner wanted Luke Harker to see the smashed radio, to have graphic proof that his compound had been violated. He wanted the self-proclaimed field marshal to feel just the slightest twinge of what so many of his victims had felt. Terror. Deathly, gut-stopping, icy cold terror.

The guy guarding the armory was lighting a cigarette. His AK-47 was clutched under one elbow. The match winked out just as a 9mm mangler entered the back of his skull and winked out the guy's own lights.

His buddy was zipping up his fly as he came around the end of the building. He saw his partner on the ground first, his brains puddled around what was left of his head, and he took two steps forward, fascinated. That's when he came upon the living shadow that materialized out of the night, the gun in its black hand a hard, real extension of death. His mouth opened in a silent O in time to take the bullet like a pill that cured whatever ailed him. For good. No more mercy. The war was on.

Bolan dragged the bodies of the two terrorists inside the unlocked armory and shut the door behind him.

A narrow-beam flashlight from his utility belt revealed the interior of the weapons storehouse. It was not empty.

The room was stacked halfway to the ceiling with enough weaponry to outfit a small army.

Most of the crates that Bolan's flash picked out were stenciled in the Russian Cyrillic alphabet. Bolan moved down an aisle, randomly taking a quick check of contents. Kalashnikov assault rifles were neatly stacked in one area, along with what had to be hundreds of thousands of rounds of 7.62mm ammunition. There were 9mm Makarov automatic pistols, complete with holsters and belts, plus a more than ample supply of a popular terrorist favorite, the Czechoslovakian Skorpion machine pistol: the compact little "room broom," light enough for one-handed firing, that could spit 7.65mm tumblers at a rate of 750 per minute.

But Bolan found the real goodies farther on. Among bazookas and Goryunov and Soviet PK-series heavy machine guns was a cache of Russian RPG-7 rocket launchers. Another set of crates held SAM-7s, the shoulder-borne ground-to-air missiles that could take out a jet by seeking the heat of its exhaust and flying up its ass: with a range of up to six miles, it could down civilian aircraft with passengers as well as low-flying fighters. There were also several batteries of radar-controlled Chilka 23mm anti-aircraft cannons.

To equip himself with this kind of arsenal, Luke Harker had to be tapped into a very special kind of pipeline.

Bolan was aware that since Mikhail Timofeyevich Kalashnikov introduced the automatic rifle that bears his name in 1947, over 40 *million* AK series weapons had been produced in Russia—and that figure did not include imitations manufactured in other Warsaw Pact nations. More AKs had been made than any other weapon of its kind in history.

And many of them had been funneled into the terrorist pipeline.

Along the way, that pipeline involved corrupt military personnel, thieves, smugglers, gunrunners, crooked customs officers. And it flowed with the blessings of heads of state—sometimes overtly, as in the case of Libya's Colonel Muammar Khaddafi, sometimes clandestinely, as in the case of Russia's leaders. And its continuity depended on the worldwide conspiracy of cooperation among the ultra-leftist terrorist groups.

A pipeline of fast, cheap, easy death.

Bolan moved catlike through the darkness, pausing occasionally to set small explosive charges. He placed most of them close to crates of grenades, incendiaries, and ammunition. Luke Harker's own munitions would help blow his wonderful compound into scorched scrap metal.

The first faint glow of dawn was creeping over the horizon as Bolan emerged. The numbers were coming down now. Bolan checked his watch, mentally set eight minutes as the outside limit of the softprobe, and moved in a half-crouch across the compound.

Opposite the armory was a double row of low prefabricated buildings facing each other across the narrow parade ground. According to Tex Hoffman, these were billets, supposedly for VIP visitors to Harker's headquarters. Each could hold up to ten men in relative comfort. As far as Tex knew they had never been used.

Evidently they were in use now.

The shadow of a parked jeep swallowed up the man in black. From that vantage point in the gray light he could see up the "street" between the billets. In front of each was a guard, and none was making any effort at getting friendly with his neighbor. Two were black, one was Oriental, several had the swarthy complexion of the Middle East, and the rest were either European or white Americans. Some wore uniforms of sorts, although each uniform was different.

Bolan did not know their identities, but he sure as hell recognized their type. Bodyguards were the same the world over, whether they were Mafia hotshots in $400 suits and gold pinky rings or Arab Fedayeen in burnooses and sandals. All of them were stolid unimaginative men who had reached their level of competence, but only just. The better ones would mindlessly give their own lives to protect the life of their boss. The others were just happy to have a job that let them carry a gun. They felt important because of it.

They did not, of course, feel so important when the gun was in someone else's hand and they were looking down the barrel.

A man came out of one of the billets. Bolan looked him over and the first pieces fell into place.

During the Mafia campaigns Mack Bolan was possessed by a relentless determination to know more about the enemy even than it knew about itself. He had compiled a mug file of known Mafiosi—a file he carried in his head. At the height of his first war he could call many hundreds of brothers of that unholy fraternity by name.

Of course, that file was much smaller now. As the first war had wound down, its prime warrior was able to pull most of the file cards and mentally mark them "deceased."

The man standing in front of the billet, not twenty meters away, held a place of honor among those who were left.

His name was Jon Carter. He was the sole survivor of that elite corps of polished mob assassins who answered only to the *capi*—who, indeed, had carte blanche, in extreme circumstances, to hit a *capo*.

Now Carter was the right-hand man of Frank Contadina, international businessman, wealthy sportsman, intimate of high society's best on two continents. Contadina was the very model of the new breed of Mafia dons.

Contadina had homes and offices in New York and London. From both cities he ran a sprawling financial conglomerate that ranged from construction firms to manufacturing to real estate investment. He owned casinos in London and Las Vegas and, through an intricate maze of holding companies and intermediaries, was the unknown but active major stockholder in several munitions firms, transportation companies, private security agencies, and two banks, one each in Zurich and Geneva.

Companies in which Contadina was involved could supply the consumer with a home, a car, or a fast-food hamburger. For another kind of consumer they could supply other items.

Items like a money-laundering service, passage from one country to another without benefit of passport or visa, even the goodwill of certain heads of state; items ranging from a crate of M-16A autorifles to a completely equipped private army.

The renascent Mafia had made a new alliance with international terrorism and both parties were finding it quite satisfactory. Frank Contadina could grow fat and sleek, and the forces of international terrorism could continue butchering the innocent and defenseless in the name of their warped ideologies.

Jon Carter was never far from Frank Contadina. Frank did not put in personal appearances in the middle of the Sahara Desert unless there was some highly compelling reason to do so.

Something very damn big was coming down here. Once again the battlefield had grown. This mission was going far beyond saving one little rich girl. Jill Breton would have to wait a while to get her butt loose of Luke Harker.

With the radio out, Harker would not find out if Harrison Breton's Project Little Bang prototype had been delivered. Therefore the girl, whatever side she was on, would be safe. And in the meantime a new battle plan had to be devised.

A new battle plan for a very old war.

A plan, basically, for a man ready to die and willing to kill. A plan fit for the chief executive in charge of justice and retribution. A plan for a raging Executioner.

7

"I want to know what's going on down there," Bolan said.

"Can't help you," Tex Hoffman shrugged. "As I said, Harker and me ain't been getting on so good lately. All I know is he's got the girl here and I was supposed to take delivery of the bomb in Algiers. Today. That's it."

Bolan unholstered the Beretta. He watched the emaciated terrorist's eyes go wide.

"Honest to God, man," Tex spluttered in fear.

"You told me those guest billets hadn't been used." Bolan dropped the magazine out of the pistol grip, drew back the slide, and lined up the notch with the dismounting latch. His hands moved firmly and surely. The motions were automatic.

"They haven't, not that I know of," Tex said.

"They're being used now," Bolan told him.

Tex's skinny face screwed up in a frown. He tugged at the brim of his Stetson. The sun had just cleared the flat desert horizon; its rays warmed the already hot air. A cloudless sky was watery blue, as bleached-out as the landscape beneath it.

"How many of Harker's men are on that base?" Bolan hammered.

"About fifty."

"There are at least two or three times that number there right now," Bolan said. "Europeans, Arabs, a few blacks and Orientals." As he spoke he wiped down the Beretta, then quickly reassembled it, pressing two fresh cartridges into the magazine before reinserting it. "What does that mean to you?"

The other man continued to shake his head.

"Once you stop talking, you stop being useful," Bolan said evenly. He chambered a 9mm Parabellum slug. Steel-jacketed judgment. "You're running out of options, guy."

"I tell you, man, I got no idea." Tex's voice trembled with panic. "That bastard down there, he's crazy, man. How the hell am I supposed to guess..." His voice trailed off in midsentence. Then he breathed, "Wait a minute."

"Keep talking, guy."

"It's crazy," Tex said, "but it could be. Harker's been going on about how he was going to run the whole shooting match someday—shit, I don't mean just lately, he's been talking that way for years. He kept saying that people were looking up to him, that they were beginning to bid for his services. There was big money passing hands, and Harker wanted a bushel of it for himself."

A composite picture of Luke Harker had been developing in Bolan's mind since the first alert from

Head Fed Hal Brognola was received at Bolan's Stony Man Farm retreat. One thing was apparent to Bolan immediately: Harker's involvement in international terrorism had as its sole motive personal enrichment.

It would be inaccurate, Bolan thought, to call Luke Harker an animal. No animal kills out of sheer greed.

"Harker kept talking about forming some kind of federation," Tex Hoffman was saying. "He claimed he could get all the groups together and set it up. Even Wolfe thought he was crazy. I never took him seriously."

"A U.N. of terror," Bolan said.

"With Harker as head honcho—as Secretary General." Tex pulled a bandana from the back pocket of his jeans and wiped his face. "The guy's a megalomaniac. Me and Wolfe, we've always known that."

Bolan opened the rear door of the Rover and began to strip weapons and armament from the blacksuit and stow them in the flight bag.

"What now, man?" Tex asked nervously.

"I'm going to find out how Harker's plans are coming along."

"How you gonna do that?"

Bolan started to unzip the blacksuit. "I'm going to ask him," he said.

8

In the early days of Mack Bolan's war against the Mafia, the man had of necessity waged a solitary fight. Sure, he considered members of the law enforcement community "soldiers of the same side," and for their part, many police officers were secretly sympathetic to Bolan's war. Often individual policemen turned their backs on his activities, consciously avoiding confrontations with the blitzing warrior. Bolan's closest friend, if any man could be said to be a friend during the long lonely years of the Mafia campaigns, was Leo Turrin, a Mafia underboss with the "girls franchise" in western Massachusetts who was in actuality an undercover Federal agent. Carl Lyons, when a Los Angeles cop, was sworn to take the man known as the Executioner dead or alive; now he was one-third of the Executioner's Able Team, fighting the common enemy. And there was Hal Brognola, the Federal agent who, instead of following his orders to stop the black-clad raider at all costs, became a willing accomplice to Bolan's highly effective cleansing action.

But essentially Mack Bolan had fought alone. His

only resources had been those he created for himself. Money to finance the war came from raids on the enemy's own treasury. Armament and other material were supplied by a network of sympathizers who knew that Bolan would protect their identities with his life if necessary. And Bolan had accepted allies only with the greatest reluctance; too many of those who had helped him died agonizing deaths for their kindness.

But now, as far as the world at large knew, Mack Bolan was dead. From the ashes of his War Wagon that had exploded one rainy Saturday in New York's Central Park had arisen Colonel John Phoenix, aka Stony Man One.

No longer was the Executioner fighting solo. Now some large and brave people stood at his side. Stony Man people like April Rose, the young woman who had backed him during the final six-day blitz that had finally gutted the Mafia underbelly: now she was "housekeeper" at his Stony Man Farm base, in total charge of security, communications, and all other support functions—including emotional support for the man she had come to love with all her heart. Aaron "the Bear" Kurtzman ran the Farm's computer control console and coordinated intelligence; using the direct link to the National Security Council's data banks, the Bear could elicit the latest info on any aspect of terrorism anywhere in the world. People like Herman "Gadgets" Schwarz and Rosario "Politician" Blancanales, one-time Vietnam

War comrades-in-arms of then Sergeant Mack Bolan, later members of the Executioner's Death Squad, now, along with Carl Lyons, his new Able Team. Gadgets Schwarz was a self-taught electronics wizard whose sophisticated designs and applications provided the basis of Stony Man Farm's communications capability. Pol Blancanales had an uncanny ability to blend into any environment and a natural gift for organization and administration; the burly Mexican-American possessed an innate understanding of psychology that bordered on clairvoyance. There was Jack Grimaldi, once a combat pilot in Vietnam, later a flyboy for the Mob, now the head of his own SOG cadre. Grimaldi could fly anything from a Piper Cub to a Boeing 747. More than once he had risked his own butt in an on-the-dime touchdown to pull his boss out of a lead hailstorm. It was Hal Brognola who was now director of the Sensitive Operations Group, the man whose duty it was to send Mack Bolan back into the hellgrounds, the man who died a little each time he did so, and who came alive a little each time the big guy came back in one piece. There was also the man to whom Hal answered—the man in the Oval Office of the White House, the man who had once confided in Brognola his opinion that Mack Bolan was "the last barricade between savagery and civilization."

There were others: Konzaki, the new armorer; Phoenix Force, the team of professional soldiers from five different countries who had already seen action in the name of Stony Man and the United States of America. For Mack Bolan it was still a lonely fight—but it was no longer one that he fought without assistance.

The technical aspects of Mack Bolan's resources as he remorselessly walked his Third Mile were extraordinary. The intelligence capabilities and records of every police agency on the local, state, and federal level were available to him, as well as those of Interpol, Britain's M16, Israel's Mossad, Germany's BND, France's Sûreté. The armory at Stony Man Farm contained the pick of the most sophisticated weapons systems in the world.

Nevertheless, when the moment came that the soft probe turned hard, when the hellfire storm began, Mack Bolan could depend on no one but himself. He was his own best intelligence, his own best kill specialist.

It was not just courage, stealth, steadiness, accuracy, the will to act without hesitation that were required for this self-sufficiency. There were also the skills of the *total* warrior, the razor-sharp instincts that the man from blood had honed over the long bloodwashed years. These instincts and styles had become weapons of a sort as well, weapons that were at times as essential as the big .44 AutoMag on Bolan's right hip.

One of these weapons Mack Bolan called "role camouflage." It could be considered a form of disguise, but it had nothing to do with masks. It consists

of representing yourself as someone you were not—
with such assurance and authority that the enemy
could not help but believe it.

The key to a successful role camouflage was an
intimate understanding of the enemy's psychological makeup. Armed with this, Mack Bolan took
advantage of the other side's preconceptions by becoming simply what they expected him to be. It was a
game of nuances, not of exaggerated stereotypes.
During the first war Mack Bolan did not expect a
sharkskin suit and an Italian accent to get him into
the Mob's boardroom. But a near-total grasp of the
criminal mind and the subtleties of criminal behavior could—and did—allow the warrior to pull it
off.

It was not a masquerade a guy should contemplate
for extended periods or capricious purposes. Mack
Bolan had survived his wars not by contempt for his
enemy but by careful respect for his cunning, and he
knew his enemies were not fools. Each penetration
was on the heartbeat. Bolan's survival in the midst of
the opposition camp depended completely on the
credibility of his every word, every gesture, every expression, every move.

Mack Bolan had still been a U.S. Army Sergeant,
then on "compassionate leave" after the deaths of
three members of his immediate family, when he first
used a form of role camouflage. Although retaining
his own identity, he presented Sergeant Bolan as a
man who had left his moral sense behind in the

jungles of Southeast Asia, a hired gun for sale to the highest bidder, uncaring to what purpose it would be put. As Bolan had surmised, this was an attitude that the Mafia jackals could understand, and it helped him infiltrate their ranks and get his bloody vengeance for what had been done to his people.

Time and again role camouflage had been a valuable aid as Bolan bored into the Mafia corpus. Equipped with a new face courtesy of a sympathetic plastic surgeon, Bolan used this "battle mask" to assume the identity of Mafia soldier Frankie Lambretta during the battle for the California hamlet of Palm Village. That identity was to come in handy again when the hellgrounds shifted to New York, Washington, and later San Diego. During the Philadelphia campaign he became one Johnny Cavaretta, a "wild card" or top-level enforcer. Using this identity, and the perpetual undercurrents of paranoia rampant in the Mob, "Cavaretta" sowed seeds of internecine suspicions that bloomed into the explosive decimation of the Mafia "family" of Don Stefano Angeletti.

Mike Blanski, Mike Borzi, B. Macklin, Stephen Ruggi, Phil Tarrantino, Frankie Vinton—all of these were at one time roles that Mack Bolan assumed to further his crusade against the Organization. Then, in the twenty-ninth campaign, in his command strike on *La Commissione*'s New York headquarters, Mack Bolan created his masterpiece of role camouflage as

"Omega." The alias came from the expression "alpha and omega," the beginning and end of the Greek alphabet. In this case Omega meant the end of the Syndicate's vise-grip on American society. The role of the near-legendary Black Ace enforcer had helped Bolan become a figure of awe and respect among the panicked remnants of the Mob. It was a masterwork of personality by sheer force. Bolan had so perfected the art of role camouflage that he was able to ride this last role creation right through that final Sabbath Day in New York when the tattered shreds of a criminal brotherhood were swept up and disposed of.

So yeah, role camouflage was another one of this warrior's skills, but one that had now gone beyond craft to become art. For Mack Bolan, it had a particularly satisfying symmetry to it, because it could never have worked, could not work now, if it did not take its strength from the enemy's essential putrefaction. It depended on the other side's weakness, spinelessness, fragmentation. It was based on the sure knowledge that any so-called "organization" composed of criminals or terrorists was actually a group of individuals out to enrich only themselves. They were banded together primarily to keep an apprehensive eye on each other.

Once again, role camouflage was about to take the battlefield philosopher back into the Beast's drooling maw.

The guy manning the gate at this fierce morning hour was an American. A casual glance would have made him as a soldier: tan fatigues, beret, Makarov automatic on his hip, AK-47 slung over his shoulder. But the glance that the Executioner gave the man was not casual. Bolan noted the scuffed boots, the uncared-for leather cracking in the heat; the holster riding too low, hotshot style; the too-flashy mirror sunglasses and the cigarette dangling from one corner of the stud's mouth. It added up to common hood.

Bolan pulled the Rover up to the gate and leaned on the horn. The guard pinched the butt from between his lips, flicked it off to one side, and took his time about coming out of the little guardhouse.

"I thought you was in Algiers," he said to Tex Hoffman, not bothering to look at Bolan.

"Harker," Bolan demanded. His voice was low and even, nearly a monotone, except for something cold and dark that made the hardman look at the stranger despite himself.

Bolan was dressed in light cotton-twill slacks, a golf shirt with a designer's symbol prominent on the breast pocket, expensive rubber-soled deck shoes, and shades in gold aviator frames. He took a folded piece of paper from the Rover's dash and held it up and repeated, "Harker."

The armed guard smiled in a twisted, sardonic way. He was going to teach this dude a few things, and he was going to enjoy giving the lesson.

"Who is this clown, Tex?" he said, and reached for the paper with his left hand.

The next part happened too fast for the tough boy to follow. All he knew was that suddenly he was bent forward over the hood of the Rover, the hot metal scorching his cheek. The "clown," still seated behind the windshield, had reached out and bent back the gunman's arm up toward his neck, sending wrenching pains through his elbow.

"Harker," Bolan said a third time, in that same emotionless voice.

It was almost like the slob was on a run of stupidity that he didn't want to break. Instead of answering he clawed clumsily at the Makarov with his free hand.

Bolan wrenched up on the arm he held. It snapped just below the elbow like a turkey's wishbone. The jagged end of the small bone of the forearm tore through the skin, glistening whitely as blood welled up around it.

The guard let out a high mewling squeal. Bolan released him and he slumped to the rock-strewn ground, lay there moaning. Bolan pulled himself out of his seat and struck the guy behind the ear with the guy's own pistol. That stopped the moaning.

Bolan took the guard's keys and tossed them to Tex, who was still sitting in the Rover. The keys fell in his lap. He stared vacantly at Bolan. There was a sickly, fear-stricken expression on his pale face.

"Move," Bolan ordered.

Tex went to the gate and his fumbling hands finally got the gate open. Bolan, behind the wheel, pulled the Rover through and waited for Tex to climb in. Without being asked, Tex pointed at the far hut to their right.

Jon Carter stood near the corner of the compound, discreetly picking remnants of breakfast out of his teeth. He was speaking with a heavyset black man in a colorful dashiki. They watched Bolan rumble past.

Luke Harker was sitting behind his desk when the man in the aviator shades came into his headquarters. Richard Wolfe was leaning forward over the desk; he was breathing a little hard, like he had just come in with something important to say.

A bodycock stood behind the two terrorists and a little to one side. He was outfitted with a 9mm Makarov and a Kalashnikov autorifle, but unlike the gateman he seemed to have some discipline about him. He brought the AK-47 around and held it loosely pointed at the floor, from which position he could bring it to bear on the intruder's midsection in a microsecond.

Jill Breton was perched on the edge of the desk with one leg drawn up. In the halter-top and short-shorts she looked like she was posing for a cheesecake photo. She gave the newcomer in the dark glasses a superior, challenging look, as if to say she had seen his kind before and was not impressed.

Wolfe stepped back from the desk. Harker merely

looked up, calmly taking in Tex Hoffman and this guy he had never seen before.

Harker opened his mouth to speak, but Bolan did not grant him the initiative. "I want to talk to you," he said. The Executioner's voice was granite hard.

"Who is this guy?" Harker asked Tex. His tone was relaxed, almost amused. This was his turf, and he controlled enough guns to keep it that way. Any ballsy bastard was no risk to him.

"You know who I am, Harker," Bolan snapped. "You know who I represent, and you've been expecting me. At least you should have been expecting me, if your head's screwed on right."

Harker reached out and stroked Jill's bare back. She smiled down at him before returning her defiant gaze to Bolan.

"If I were you, mister," Harker drawled, "I'd start by explaining what you're talking about. Seems to me, barging in here like this, you could be in a tight spot if you weren't very careful."

"You're the one on the spot, Harker."

Wolfe cleared his throat. "Excuse me. My name is . . ."

"Richard Wolfe," Bolan cut in. His tone was outright rude.

"And you're . . . ?"

" 'Stone' will do," Bolan said. Sure, Stone, as in Stony Man.

"Wonderful," Harker said sardonically, still seated. Bolan gave him a hard look. Harker kept the leer pasted to his face, but Bolan could see it cost him some effort. Evidently he was beginning to see things in this scene he did not like.

"What can we do for you, Stone?" Wolfe asked.

"Wait a minute," Harker interjected, glaring at "Stone." "Why don't you answer *me* one question—who the fuck do you think you are?"

Bolan took a couple steps forward and leaned over Harker, ignoring the girl a half-foot away. He placed both hands palm-down on the terrorist "field marshal's" desk.

"I'm here to apologize for killing those four boys of yours in Algiers," he said. It sounded like no apology at all.

The girl gasped. Harker's high shiny cheekbones went beet red, but for a moment he did not move. Bolan's gaze had him pinned to the spot like an insect on a board. Then he jerked upright and transfixed Tex Hoffman with his own gaze.

"What the goddamn hell is he talking about?"

Tex swallowed. "Fahmeer was on the front door," he said in a thin voice. "Stone got him coming in, and then he got Amahl, Makir, and Billy C. upstairs."

"And why didn't *you* get him?"

"Why do you think, Harker?" Bolan cut in. "My people wanted me to talk to you. Fast. To talk to you I had to find you. Hoffman here knew where you were. To talk to Hoffman I had to kill a few of your boys."

"You found me," Harker said, shaking his head slowly, his eyes still wide. "So you found me . . ."

Bolan brought a pack of smokes to his mouth, pulled out a cigarette with his lips, lit it and dropped the match on the floor. Jill was still looking at him, but her arrogant expression was now replaced by open curiosity.

"There's a lot of territory out there," Bolan began. "Enough for everyone, so long as nobody gets greedy. My people think maybe you're getting greedy."

"Tough shit," Luke Harker said. Wolfe blinked nervously.

Bolan blew out smoke and grinned rather sadly, like he genuinely was sorry for the guy. "You know, Harker," he said slowly, "you really are a dumb fuck."

Harker's head snapped back with surprise. The movement was so sudden that the bodycock behind him started bringing up his AK-47.

Bolan pressed on. "Here you are, sitting in the middle of the desert, in a tin shack with not enough air conditioning, calling yourself 'field marshal' and playing soldier. The men I'm talking about are sitting in big offices in big cities. Some of those big cities are seats of government. And what these men call themselves, they really are, and you can believe in them."

Jill was watching him with continued interest.

"These men have two complaints," Bolan said.

"One, they think you might be trying to step into places where they've staked first claim. They don't like thinking that. It makes them nervous, and when these men get nervous, other men get dead." Bolan grinned again. "It could happen to anyone, Harker.

"Second is the matter of this girl here."

Bolan watched Jill's eyes widen with astonishment. He was glad to see it. It suggested that she was unaware of Harker's nuclear extortion scheme. She had no idea she was so important.

"Trying to get to Breton through his daughter is nothing less than idiotic," Bolan drove on. He was working Harker like a boxer who had his opponent on the ropes. He was hitting him now with some good punches, determined to end it before another round. The idea of this first psychological drive was to push the guy as close to his limit as possible without exceeding it.

Exceeding it would come later.

"That little nuclear bomb you're trying to lay hands on is a U.S. government project," Bolan told him, "and you don't mess with them, not with the kind of fucked-up scheme you're trying to pull. When the heat comes down on any one group in our business, it comes down on everyone, directly or indirectly."

Harker was nearing the boiling point. It was a bad time for Jill to speak.

"Luke," she said, "what is he talking about?"

"Shut up."

"You told me—you said we were going to work together."

"Shut up!" Harker roared. He grabbed her arm and she half-fell, her eyes charged suddenly with terror. Bolan didn't like to see this happen to her, but the entire mission—which included her safety—depended on him maintaining his camouflage.

"Get this bitch out of here," Harker ordered his bodycock, but Jill darted through the back door before anyone could push her around any more. The guard followed her and a moment later they heard the sound of kicking, a squeal, the click of a door being locked; the man returned alone.

Harker was shaking with rage and confusion. "You got any more to say?"

"Just one thing," Bolan sneered. "You'd be a lot better off with as few brains as you've got balls."

Harker sprang to his feet, his face a mottled red and purple. "Look, asshole—" he thundered.

Bolan backhanded him hard across the face.

The bodycock stepped forward and closed the muzzle of the Kalashnikov in on the big man. "Hold it," Richard Wolfe said quickly. No one else moved.

Luke Harker reached up one hand and rubbed at his face, his look distorted with shock. Mack Bolan eyed the guard, ready to go for the automatic pistol nestled in the back of his belt.

A young soldier burst through the door behind Bolan.

"Pardon me, sir," said the newcomer nervously,

aware of the tension that hung like a pall of smoke. Also he was bearing bad news; his nervousness was nearing breaking point.

"What is it?" Harker shouted.

The young kid glanced at Bolan.

"What the fuck is it?" Harker yelled.

"The two men assigned to armory security detail are dead, sir," the guy said quickly. "Shot. Also, the radio transceiver has been wrecked. I don't think it can be fixed. The guy whacked Sparks over the head. The medic says he'll be okay, but right now he's still out cold."

"Get out of here," Harker said through clenched teeth.

"Yes, sir." The kid disappeared.

"Looks like this isn't going to be your day." Bolan glanced at his watch. "And it's not even ten yet."

"Shut up."

"I'll tell you what I think," Bolan went on. "I think your little Woodstock for terrorists isn't all unity and brotherhood. I think someone's already trying to cut in on your action."

Bolan turned away from him, letting Harker get a look for the first time at the little .38 automatic tucked in his waistband. "Let's go, Hoffman."

"Wait a minute," Harker said. "Where do you think you're going?"

"Wherever."

"You've delivered your message, Stone. Now I

want you *off my base*.'' He was exhaling fumes of fury.

Bolan turned to stare at Harker. Behind him Tex got the door open, ready to beat a hasty retreat.

''I'm going to give you one last piece of advice, free of charge,'' Bolan told Harker. ''You learn to keep a lock on that mouth of yours. Especially don't try to tell me what to do.''

''You can't—''

''If you want to even the score, you go right ahead. Any time you grow the legs to try it.''

Bolan turned his back on Harker and did not bother to close the door when he exited.

Sweat was streaming off Tex Hoffman's face.

Bolan had gotten his message across, loud, clear, and nine-by-nine.

Fear and suspicion were like a boulder rolling off a mountaintop. It took some pushing to get it started, but once there it took its energy from its own momentum. That's what had started happening now. And it would take a lot of other boulders with it.

Of course, the end of the ride was abrupt.

And violent.

But for the winner there was an unusual pleasure. The sight of losers crushed by an avalanche of their own worst fears. Smashed by the accumulated lunacy of their paranoia and worst imaginings.

Bolan could almost feel it. It was certainly worth the very real risk of death.

Role camouflage was strictly front line stuff. If

you didn't like it, you crawled fast under the nearest rock.

If you could take it, if you could stand to push a killer to the very brink and then shove him off in front of all his friends, then you should play it to the hilt.

For Bolan, it was worth it every time.

9

Mack Bolan had what psychologists call an "eidetic memory." The term refers to an extraordinary ability to recall visual images and their significance in detail. Most people know it as a photographic memory.

The Executioner had used the skill to develop a mental mug file filled with the visages of known terrorists, the listings growing as his New War progressed. He did not remember individual names in every case, since many of them were in unfamiliar languages. But Bolan could accurately match the man with his organization, and in most cases place the face within that organization's hierarchy.

Now as Bolan/Stone stalked through the terrorist basecamp with a nerve-wracked Tex Hoffman at his side, many of those familiar faces stared back at him.

Bolan could sense keenly the tension in the wretchedly hot air. Despite the unmerciful sun, men were out of their air-conditioned billets, like restive animals uneasy in their lairs. They stood in small groups or strolled uncomfortably around the compound, mostly staying to themselves. Several were checking out Harker's facilities while making studious efforts to appear uninterested.

Bolan nodded at a small group of men in fatigues in front of the nearest billet. They stared back stonily, then turned away. Bolan lit a cigarette and leaned against the jeep that had served as cover during his softprobe just a few hours earlier. The pose successfully conveyed the impression that the man was at ease in this pained crowd.

"Jesus Christ," Tex moaned at his elbow, his voice vibrant with fear. "Harker pulled it off, didn't he?"

Apparently, yeah, he had. The guy was a megalomaniac, and probably certifiably insane as well, for what that was worth. But he had managed what even his two right-hand men thought was a pipe dream, something that had been attempted but never before accomplished so completely in the twilight world of terror.

Luke Harker had brought representatives of every major terrorist organization in the world to the middle of the Sahara Desert for a convocation of death.

Bolan scanned the men loitering around, mentally cataloging affiliations, nationalities, loyalties. One of the larger delegations was a coalition of groups aligned under the Palestinian Liberation Organization banner.

A number of the faces were on Bolan's mental roster of the Popular Front for the Liberation of Palestine. One of the most violent of the PLO groups, the PFLP was also one of the longest-lived. Its first big operation involved Algeria itself, when in 1968 the PFLP hijacked an Israeli El Al airliner to Algiers. For the next five weeks thirty-two civilian Jewish passengers, innocent of any involvement and victimized solely for their religion and nationality, were held hostage before negotiations were complete. Hijacking then became a favorite PFLP tool. During the following months the group commandeered thirteen more planes, including four in one single operation. On that occasion three of the planes were blown up while on the ground in Jordan, considered a "moderate" nation. The PFLP claimed additional responsibility for the destruction of a Swissair plane in flight, killing all forty-seven passengers and crew on board. It made Bolan enraged beyond anger, into pure fury.

Also present in the compound were representatives of Fatah, a group that claimed the life of a United States ambassador and two other Western diplomats when it overran the Saudi embassy in Sudan in 1973. The Syrian Palestinian group As Saiqa was represented by its grandly named wing, The Eagles of the Revolution, which had recently demonstrated revolutionary commitment by kidnapping an elderly unarmed Jordanian diplomat in protest against King Hussein's peace-keeping efforts. It was another vivid reminder to Mack Bolan that peace is the *last* thing any terrorist desires.

PLO groups were responsible for two of the most

despicable acts of modern terrorism, setting off streams of noble human blood that stained the whole world and earned for them forever the enmity of Mack Bolan. The first was in 1972, when guerrillas representing themselves as members of a group called Black September massacred eleven Israeli athletes at the 1972 Munich Olympics, an international occasion set aside for nations to gather in peaceful athletic competition. And Bolan remembered only too well the damnable sequel: when Abu Daoud, leader of the Munich raid, was captured in France in 1976, neither France nor West Germany would prosecute, for fear that vital oil supplies might be cut off in retaliation. Daoud was released in one day and flown first class to that ever-popular terrorist refuge, Algiers.

The second notorious PLO operation had a more just conclusion. This was the now-famous hijacking of a French Airbus to the airport at Entebbe, Uganda, in 1976 by a mixed team of German and Palestinian terrorists. But this time a crack squad of Israeli commandos, specially trained for just this type of contingency, attacked almost immediately, killing or capturing the hijackers and liberating their hostages, among them several Americans.

In other words, the Israelis did not miss their shot. That was the sort of response Mack Bolan approved of. Action, swift and deadly, was the only answer to terrorists' demands. Shoot first.

Bolan flicked his cigarette butt into the dirt and moved casually up the open space between the two rows of billets. Men looked at him, but most turned their eyes away quickly from his steady gaze. Bolan's plan called for making an impression, letting his presence be known. He wanted dangerous, frightened, avaricious people to wonder just who he was allied with, whose side he was on, what threat to their own selfish plans he posed. The more they wondered about him, the more they were going to wonder about each other. And thus things got rolling.

Further down the line of billets Bolan recognized representatives of several groups that had occasionally done "favors" for the Palestinians. There was the German Baader-Meinhof Gang, which teamed up with Black September to demonstrate its perverted notion of "humanity" by killing seven residents of a Jewish old persons' home in Munich. Bolan also noted several members of the Rengo Sekigun, or Japanese Red Army. Three commandos from this group were responsible for the shooting up of a crowded terminal room in Israel's Lod airport, resulting in twenty-six killed and seventy-two wounded. Sixteen of the dead were Americans.

Any comraderie among the groups was rapidly and visibly eroding in this place. Word had gotten out about the dead guards, the smashed radio, no doubt the dead patrol, certainly the presence in camp of this mysterious man in the dark aviator glasses. Everyone would be making damned sure of a sudden to cover his own butt.

"Very smooth, Mr. Stone."

Bolan turned. So did Tex. It was Jon Carter. Bolan ignored the hand that the Mafia Ace proffered.

"I'm—"

"I know who you are," Bolan said.

Carter lowered his hand. Carter was a highly skilled killer with enough brains to keep a handle on anything that could endanger himself or his boss, Contadina. Bolan assumed the slick Ace was working on that handle right now.

"What else do you know, Mr. Stone?" Carter said amiably.

"Let me put it this way," Bolan told him. "My people—"

"Who are your people, Stone?"

"Don't be a jerk, Carter."

The other man broadened his smile and shrugged.

"You know goddamn well, because you do business with them all the time," Bolan said. "My people are happy with the relationship, and that's why I'm going to give you some advice."

"I'd appreciate that."

"Luke Harker has bitten off more than he can chew here. You know that. It's going to blow up in his face. So make sure you don't get caught at ground zero."

"That's it?" But Carter's true concern was betrayed by his distant look, as if he was giving the big guy's words some serious consideration. "I want you to meet someone," he said suddenly, coming to a decision.

Bolan shrugged.

"I'd rather you were alone."

"Hey, that's okay," Tex put in. "I can just, uh...."

"He's with me," Bolan told Carter. Tex rolled his eyes upward, then joined the two of them as they moved toward Carter's billet.

The air conditioning made entering it like leaping into a pool of ice water. It was easily fifty degrees cooler inside than out.

The windows were shaded and the only light was what filtered through. The room was surprisingly well-furnished. A long modern-looking davenport was set along one wall with a portable bar next to it. Luke Harker was taking good care of his VIP guests.

A man sitting at the far end of the davenport was obscured by the shadows. He did not move when they came in, but the man next to him came to his feet.

"I don't need to meet Contadina," Bolan said to Carter, deliberately omitting the "mister."

"Harker told me about you, Stone," said the man who was standing. He was in his mid-fifties, nearly bald but very tanned and fit, a man who took care of himself. This was Contadina.

"So?" said Bolan.

"Would you like to make some money?"

"Sure."

"Get me out of here."

Bolan laughed.

"Will you do it?"

"No," Bolan said. Contadina was scared. Interesting. That fit in so well with Bolan's plans for the guy.

"Shit," Contadina muttered.

"There's nothing to worry about, Mr. Contadina," Jon Carter said. "Look, why don't you go lie down for a while?"

"If I wanted to lie down, I'd be doing it already."

"My people didn't send me out here to play nurse maid to you, Contadina," Bolan said. "That's Carter's job. You better hope he can handle it."

For the first time Bolan saw some heat in the glare the urbane Carter cast at him. Good. He was getting to this guy too.

"I'm going to my room," Contadina said. "Have someone bring me a fucking drink." He exited and slammed the door behind him.

Bolan gave Carter a wide grin. "You're wasting my time, Carter," Bolan needled. "You're going to have to baby-sit Contadina on your own." Behind him Tex edged toward the door, hoping like hell to get out of there.

"That's not why I asked you in here," Carter said evenly.

The man sitting at the shadowy end of the davenport had not yet moved—Bolan had kept an eye on him since entering the room. Now he drew himself languidly to his feet and came to where they were standing, his face still hidden in shadow until he was in front of Bolan.

Physically he wasn't particularly impressive. He was almost baby-faced. He wore a mustache that drooped past the corners of his mouth and his thick dark hair was wavy and shiny with some kind of dressing. His build was dense, compact; he had a bull-like chest.

But what struck Bolan most about the man was his eyes. They were dark, the pupils a little too small, and they were utterly blank, completely devoid of any expression or emotion, almost inanimate. If a man's eyes are the window to his soul, then the opacity of this man's eyes only disguised the fact that he had no soul at all.

Bolan said, "Hello, Rikki."

He had never met the guy before, nor had he seen the guy's photograph. None was known to exist. But two eyewitness descriptions were stored in the Stony Man Farm computer data banks.

Each had gone on at length about those blank eyes.

So Bolan knew the guy, yeah.

Knew he was a passionless killer directly responsible for the deaths of well over two hundred innocent people during dozens of operations that had set new degrees of callous malevolence. And the bastard did not even pretend to an ideology. He was a mercenary, a hired gun exacting huge cuts of the booty that his kidnappings, hijackings, and extortion schemes realized for his terrorist masters. That was how it worked these days.

Now he was here, in the billet of a Mafia *capo*, in the compound of a would-be terrorist ringleader.

Bolan returned the man's hollow gaze and the last number dropped into place.

It added up to a three-way confederation of mobster, mercenary, and megalomaniac allied to implement a plan for worldwide terror.

Except for one thing.

Mack Bolan had decided to change the geometry.

The Executioner was about to bring some new math into the ageless dead lands of the desert.

10

Although Ricardo Roybal was born in Mexico, he had in his possession at various times passports identifying him as "Humphrey Clarke" of Great Britain, "Pierre St. Jacques" of Belgium, "Ali ben-Saud" of Libya, "Peter Miller" of Chicago.

But to the police of four continents he was known simply as Rikki the Hyena.

Reportedly he had made up the nickname himself, taking no offense at the implication that he was a scavenger of carrion.

His father, a physician, professed a lifelong devotion to the cause of communism, which did not keep him from becoming one of the wealthiest men in Mexico City. Although indoctrinating his son in Marxism from the time he was a child, Dr. Roybal also sent him to one of the best preparatory schools in England, where Rikki first made contact with the ultra-left wing of the student movement.

The name of Ricardo Roybal first appeared in the files of U.S. intelligence agencies in the late sixties, when a Cuban defector provided a list of foreigners present at that time in Castro's terrorist training facility, Camp Matanzas, located just outside Havana. Rikki was enrolled in the standard curriculum: forgery, disguise, extortion, sabotage, weaponry, arson, assassination. The camp supervisor was a KGB agent, and it was during Rikki's training there that he was first recruited to do field work for the Russian agency. Apparently Rikki passed the tryout, because he was sent on for further training at the infamous Patrice Lumumba University in Moscow, where a student body of over 20,000 foreigners is continually indoctrinated in the cant of Soviet communism.

After graduation from Lumumba U, Rikki's career truly blossomed. His Russian masters realized that in Rikki they had the perfect instrument of terror: the short, round-faced, seemingly innocuous Mexican was a remorseless killing machine, devoid of ideology, loyalty, or morality, devoted only to whoever paid him well to practice his deadly skills.

Rikki's connection to the KGB had never been severed completely. Rikki the Hyena knew as well as anyone that the only "retirement" from the Russian agency was a bullet in the back of the head, so he continued to do the Soviets' bidding when called upon. But he knew that more lucrative employment was available by selling his skills on a freelance basis.

For several years he had worked on contract for Wadi Haddad, founder of the Popular Front for the Liberation of Palestine. A peaceful Israeli agricultural kibbutz near the Syrian border; the Israeli embassy in a democratic European capital; a meeting of concentration camp survivors in a small German town—all were victims of attacks organized by Rikki the Hyena. Nearly eighty people died in these three attacks alone.

Rikki began to rent his services to other groups; the murder of a Spanish government official, on a contract from the Basque separatist ETA; the hijacking of a plane carrying three OPEC oil ministers, at the request of the PLO; the bombing of a Swiss bank; the kidnapping of an Italian army officer; the assassination of the president of a small pro-Western African nation; the list went on and on.

And it was as if Rikki's very audacity protected him. The closest he had ever come to capture was several years earlier in Paris, when he was caught with three others in a famous surprise raid on a terrorist safehouse. The police did not know that one of those cornered was Rikki the Hyena until he pulled a sneak-gun and blasted his way out of the trap, killing two *gendarmes* in the process.

No photograph had ever been positively identified as depicting the terrorist mercenary. Two confessed terrorists had, on separate occasions, provided detailed verbal descriptions of the Hyena. Both were found dead in their jail cells within a week, one stabbed, the other strangled.

Today Ricardo Roybal was known to have taken on another client: the new international Mafia.

When possible, Mack Bolan preferred to choose

his arena of battle, to pick his time for engaging the enemy. But sometimes he did not have that luxury, and instinct from years of living on the heartbeat took over.

This time the situation was primed as never before. The time to strike was now, and the battlefield had to be right here, in this terrorist-ridden camp in the middle of the nowhere African desert.

The kill-zone was ready. It awaited the opening thrust.

"Thanks for the introduction," Bolan said curtly. He turned on his heel, Tex Hoffman eagerly tailing him to the door. Bolan stopped and looked back at the other two men. There was an insecure smile of fear on Jon Carter's face, but the visage of Rikki the Hyena remained utterly expressionless.

"My, uh... *people* are going to find this cocktail party very interesting," Bolan announced. "You can count on hearing from them—if you can get out of here with your heads still on your shoulders."

Dolan gave Carter a curt nod and went out into the broiling sunshine. He smiled to himself. He remembered that time like yesterday: that time when his Mafia targets were left as just heads. No bodies. Just heads.

He was playing with fear in full gear now. This was righteous justice. Ironically it was the Communist theoretician Friedrich Engels who wrote over one hundred years ago that terror "is for the most part useless cruelties perpetrated by people who are themselves frightened, for the purpose of reassuring themselves.'' Then he would frighten them mightily, from the chill, nagging fear whose cold touch actually drove the terrorists on in their pursuit of power and possession, through to the final fireball of retribution that would bring them at last to the home fires of hell.

"Man, I never saw nothing like you," Tex Hoffman said. "Luke Harker, he knows how to twist people around, but he's Captain Kangaroo compared." Tex squinted uncomfortably into the relentless sun. "Who *are* you, man?"

"I'm getting asked that a lot today."

"Listen," Tex said urgently, "you got what you wanted, so let's split. My stomach feels like I swallowed a handful of iron filings, and I gotta—" He cut himself off and turned, if possible, even more pale. "Aw shit," he said passionately.

Bolan watched through his aviator shades as Luke Harker strode across the compound toward them, accompanied by the ever-present hardmen. Bolan had spent years in the humid tropical rain forests of Southeast Asia, so the dry desert heat was not especially oppressive to him. He noticed that Harker had also acclimatized himself. His uniform was crisp and clean, despite a temperature that had to be near 110 degrees and creeping higher.

"You given any thought to what I said?" Bolan called to Harker.

"This is my territory, mister," Harker replied. His voice was controlled. "You've been snooping around for the better part of an hour. You been holed up with that wop Contadina, and Carter and his little playmate—I guess you met him."

"Maybe."

"I want you out of here," Harker said. "Now. Or I kill you myself."

"I'll tell my wise men that was your answer," Bolan said pleasantly. "Come on, Tex."

"He stays."

Bolan could smell animal fear radiating off Tex Hoffman.

"Get in the Rover, Hoffman," Bolan said evenly, his gaze daring Harker to object.

Behind Bolan, Tex scrambled across the pebbly ground to the vehicle, almost falling. Bolan heard the rig's door slam shut.

Bolan grinned sourly at Harker and turned his back on the guy.

11

Richard Wolfe was pacing the floor of Harker's office like a caged animal. The goddamn air conditioning couldn't keep him from sweating. This was the last time he was ever going to come out to this shithole desert, Wolfe vowed, whatever Harker said.

The afternoon heat was only one of several things that Wolfe had on his mind, but it sure as hell made it harder to concentrate on the others.

First, there was the international mob that Harker had brought into the camp. A shoot-out between the Turkish contingent and the Armenian crowd could happen at any time. He knew about those guys. He knew that all of the delegations had one thing in common with Luke Harker: they were in this game for themselves, and they'd stop at nothing to carve as big a piece of personal territory as possible.

Second was this guy who called himself Stone. That was not necessarily his name, of course. These guys, all of them, they took new names—even new faces—so often they probably forgot who they'd once been. Wolfe had heard about guys like Stone, men who moved like ghosts through the shadowland of the highest echelons of international terrorism, men who pulled strings that these others jokers wandering around here had no idea even existed. Stone was an independent with no allegiance to any one movement, only to those men, wherever they were, who long ago had accomplished more even than Luke Harker was attempting now. Only Rikki was blank enough not to be fazed by him in an instant.

Third, Richard Wolfe was worried about Harker himself.

Once, years before, Wolfe had hired a team of private detectives to find out what they could about Harker's early years. Wolfe figured that if anything went really wrong, such knowledge could give him an edge over his partner. The men Wolfe hired were very good at what they did.

They found that Harker was brought up by wealthy parents in a community in southern Connecticut, an hour by commuter train from New York City. He went to a private day school and then to a prep school in western Massachusetts. His grades were generally mediocre and he was a constant disciplinary problem, so after he was expelled from the prep school in his freshman year his parents sent him to a military academy in North Carolina.

Around this time, Harker began psychiatric treatment that would continue on and off throughout his teenage years. He was considered a highly intelligent young man, with an I.Q. around 150 that was not reflected in his school grades. The root of his difficulties lay in the fact that he was what one doctor called "an emotional extremist." He lacked the ability to control and limit his emotions: love, hate, jealousy, aggression, vengeance. Although this ability is a learned one, without it the chance of acquiring inhibition in later life is remote, especially in the kind of life arranged for Luke and his ilk by their parents' affluence and attendant disengagement in parenting.

By the time Wolfe got to hook up with Harker in the late 1960s, the man's anti-social behavior had taken focus. The protest movement of that time gave a guy like Harker a golden opportunity for all the attention he could handle.

The media called it charisma. Wolfe, something of a cynic, called it mass hypnotism. Whatever it was, Harker always had, and retained, an intense ability to overpower people, to control and influence and manipulate them, with his power and with his paranoia.

But now Harker was playing in the big leagues. These weren't a bunch of brainless rich-kid college students. Maybe he wasn't used to this. He was acting like a spoiled kid, on the verge of psychotic tantrums. Wolfe knew that if he didn't snap out of it real soon they were both in deep water.

Getting deeper.

Luke Harker came into the office from the door behind his desk, tucking his shirt into his khaki pants. He threw Wolfe a witless grin.

"The word's got around about the radio and the two dead guards," Wolfe pointed out, and was perversely pleased to see a little of his boss's satisfaction fade.

"Well, what are you saying?" muttered Harker.

"I'm saying that Stone or someone here is trying to blow this whole conference right out of the water. You've got nearly one hundred and fifty visitors on base, Luke, and very few who haven't done a whole bunch of killing in their time."

"Double the regular patrols," Harker said briskly. "I want our men visible and moving throughout the compound until the meeting tonight. Set up the machine guns in the guard towers. Form the remaining men into three- or four-man plainclothes squads. Make sure each squad has more than one language among them. See, it ain't Stone. I know it."

"I'll take care of it," Wolfe said. "How about the girl?"

Harker called for one of his bodycocks. The gunman entered and Harker gave him a signal. The man exited and a moment later reappeared with Jill Breton. She was standing upright, but if the guard had not been gripping one of her arms tightly she would have collapsed to the floor. Her eyes were half-open, doped; there was a bruise on one cheek and a worm of dried blood at the corner of her mouth. Her blond hair was knotted and tangled. A dirty sheet was draped over her shoulders, but it had fallen open in the front. Wolfe took his time feasting his eyes on the rich swell of her full breasts, the triangle of soft blond down between her thighs.

Harker reached over and pulled the girl into his lap, grinning at Wolfe like some drunken country boy as he did so. The sheet fell away entirely. The girl tried to say something. All that emerged was a moan. Harker let his hands rove over the naked girl, kneading hard at her soft flesh.

"What have you got her on?" Wolfe asked.

"Just a little, oh...call it a sedative," Harker replied. His hand moved lower on the girl's body. "You seen enough?" he leered.

The guard took the drugged girl out of the room. Wolfe waited until she was gone, then insisted, "We've got to make a decision about her."

"Without the radio we got no way of knowing if her old man came through with that little package we been waiting on."

"Frankly, I think we have bigger things to worry about."

Harker leaned back in his swivel chair. "Nothing's bigger than a nuclear bomb. Anyway, she's not doing us any harm."

"Yes, she is. You heard what Stone said."

"Fuck Stone," Harker spat. "I say we might still be able to use the girl. I know *I've* found a use for her...."

"You'd better keep your mind on the meeting."

Harker's leer broadened. "I'm thinking about after the meeting."

"She's outlived her usefulness," Wolfe counseled. "Either the bomb is sitting in Algiers already or it isn't going to be delivered. The deadline is two hours past. Either way she isn't going to do us much good, am I right?"

"Maybe she ain't going to do *you* any good, Dickie boy."

"I'm worried about Stone," Wolfe persisted, "partly because everything he said makes sense. We could be in some trouble, and I tell the truth."

The good humor had drained from Harker's face. When he spoke his voice was low and cold.

"The guy's gone, Richard, so forget him. From here on, everything goes tick, tick, tick. No more guards getting chewed up, no more fights, everything just like we figured. In a few hours I'm going into that meeting hall and I'm going to show those assholes. Then your buddy Stone can go screw himself up a tree, because 'his people' are going to be pleased to kiss my ass just to get permission to blow their fucking noses. Can you appreciate this?"

If it were true, that he had nothing to worry about, thought Wolfe bitterly, then why am I so worried all the time? He left the prefabricated office quarters, and once again the super-heated desert air literally staggered him. If he spent the rest of his life here, he would never ever get used to it.

He crossed the compound toward the TWPLF barracks, to order the beefed-up patrol details.

He felt that someone was following him. He

stopped and looked around. It was that bastard Stone. No doubt about it.

Wolfe was getting seriously rattled.

He'd better move it with those patrols.

12

Mack Bolan had redonned the blacksuit to become, again, one with his brother the night.

Under the daylight glare of the desert sun the kit would have been an obvious liability, soaking up heat like a sponge. Now, just after dusk, it was an invaluable asset.

The latest in a long line of combat suits that Bolan had worn into battle, the blacksuit now was for nighttime anywhere. He had designed the first blacksuit himself back in the early Mafia campaigns, incorporating features that made it more than just a garment. The fit was skintight, nothing to snag or otherwise impede the means of death; impediment could mean his life. The slit pockets were designed to hold the variety of armament that Bolan took to war. They were strategically placed for instant and easy access. Because the war was wherever he was.

The purpose of the black hue was twofold. First, the coloration was protective, the shadows of darkness for a silent nightfighter. But equally important was the psychological purpose. It stopped people in their tracks. The sudden appearance of the apparition in black caused men to hesitate. And that got them killed.

Over the years of warfare the skinsuit had become almost a part of Bolan's body. His hands went to its pockets instinctively, without conscious thought, and his movements became entirely catlike as he prowled through the darkness.

The desert/arctic nightsuit he wore in the Saharan evening now had been designed to Stony Man's specifications by the same group that designed the protective clothing for NASA's astronauts. The team included a psychologist, a physician specializing in musculature and bone structure, and a chemical engineer, among others. The suit was made of a space-age fabric, highly elastic and rip-resistant. Chemical properties made it cool in summer climates, warm in winter; folded double it acted as an emergency survival blanket.

The Executioner was rigged for light combat. Firepower came from the 9mm Belle under his left arm and the Ingram M-10 hanging from a lanyard around his neck, the total machine pistol for what had to be done. Both weapons were silenced. Too, the folding wire stock had been removed from the Ingram for extra mobility.

This was to be a surreptitious infiltration. Bolan did not intend to advertise his presence. But he had to have Big Thunder, the .44 AutoMag pistol, riding his right hip as backup.

Completing the blitzer's equipment roster, in a

small chest pack, Bolan carried a remote radio transmitter set to the frequency that would detonate the explosives he had planted during his softprobe of the early morning.

The cut Bolan had made previously in the chainlink fence was as he had left it, the links overlapped so that only a close inspection would reveal the breach in Harker's perimeter. Clearly his troops were none too observant in the unpleasant conditions of the desert. Bolan reopened the gap and slipped through in the darkness.

The summit was to start in a little more than an hour.

The Japanese guy was whistling as he came leaning around the corner. The hardman was big for a Japanese, nearly as tall as Bolan and broad in the shoulders. He went on whistling as the man all in black loomed up before him. His mouth opened in a toothy grin, and he took another step forward.

Then his right foot slashed upward in a karate kick, the limb moving incredibly fast for a man his size.

The body was in midair when a pencil of silent flame squirted from the business end of the Beretta. The 9mm organ-shredder caught the Japanese in the middle of the chest, the impact halting his forward motion so that he flopped heavily on his bent knees and back at Bolan's feet.

Bolan was familiar with that kick. The flat of the

heel of the foot can slam into the point of the nose and drive it upward at an angle, impelling splinters of bone and cartilage past the sinus cavities and into the brain's frontal lobes.

Neat. Quiet. Clean.

Bolan waited until another human shape appeared, then said, "Over here."

An Irish terrorist paused uncertainly, peering into the shadows. He took one step toward where Bolan waited.

He died staring sightlessly through vacant eyes. A stiletto stuck out of his chest just below the breastbone. The nightfighter had not forgotten the Fairbairon-Sykes combat blade. This was the right part of the world for it. Many an Arab in Algiers can stick a man's eye at forty feet. In fact what they liked to do a lot was to remove a tourist's finger with a single upward slice, to secure the ring there. Bolan lowered the man gently to the arid ground.

He did not have to wait for further action. He heard the crunch of bootsteps in the gravel.

Bolan grabbed a fistful of fatigues at the throat. A pinned South American psycho tried to knee him in the crotch and bring up his sidearm at the same time.

Bolan jammed the silencer of the Beretta into the guy's gut and triggered it. The soft *pfut* was heavily muffled by the guard's body. The only sound was the soft cracking of bone and the gush of intestines and minced flesh spewing out of the exit wound in the small of the guy's back. His last fetid breath expelled in Bolan's face as his back belched fragments. He fell from the Executioner's arms, a bubbling sack.

Bolan eased back into the shadows and checked the luminous dial of his watch. The numbers were half up, and they'd go all to hell when the first body was discovered. It was quiet now. Without hesitation, he moved off after Jill Breton. Action was everything. No more waiting. No more planning. But more killing—almost certainly.

The front room of Luke Harker's billet was brightly lit. Through the window Bolan saw Harker's two guards. One was playing solitaire at Harker's desk, listless. The other was on his feet, balancing a throwing knife in his right palm. The arm cocked back, the knife was gone, a wrist flicked quickly. The knife was imbedded in the wooden door at chest height. The bodycock crossed the room, retrieved his blade, then set for another practice throw.

The rest of the billet was dark, except for the rear corner room. Muted red light seeped out around drawn shades. Bolan crouched, moved into the shadow beneath the window. For a moment the only sound was the whirr of the sash-mounted air-conditioning unit over Bolan's head. Then he heard a woman's scream.

It dissolved into a ragged giggle. But there was no joy, only the knife-edge of caged hysteria in that unnatural laughter. Bolan moved away.

He waited until he heard the sound of the knife hitting the door again, and then the creaking of the wood as the blade was pulled free. He counted two beats. He hit the door hard.

The knifeman spun as Bolan came bursting through. He threw underhanded, the motion sure and fluid. The guy was good and he was fast.

The Executioner was better and faster.

The knife stabbed into the wall where Bolan's throat had been a millisecond before. Bolan himself was not interested in past history. The Ingram machine pistol was in his hands, embraced by his palms, the barrel tracking onto the knifeman.

The burst of eight 9mm rippers arrived at the guy's lower gut and stitched diagonally upward across his chest. A red mist surrounded the dead man's jerking body. The air was filled with the myriad streams of one late human being's blood.

One of the slugs, or part of it, had nailed the other guard as he sat. There was a small ragged hole high up on one cheek. Blood dripped from it onto the cards of his solitaire layout.

His eyes were wide as he faced Bolan, but he saw nothing. The man was blind. The ricochet had severed his optic nerves. He was groping for the stock of his AK-47. His fingers found it and closed over it.

Bolan approached, laid the hot muzzle of the M-10 against the guy's temple and ended him for good with a single mercy round.

The door behind the dead man opened into a short

hall. As Bolan stepped into the hall, the door at the other end of it opened and Luke Harker came out. He was wearing shorts only. In his fist he held a Luger.

Bolan shot him in the right foot.

Harker's eyes went wide with pain and the Luger dropped as he tumbled clumsily to the rough floorboards. In the dim light of the hallway, all he could make out was a big guy in black standing right over him. He started to howl in animal rage and terror.

Bolan slammed the barrel of the Ingram against the side of Harker's head. The scream choked on itself. An ugly gurgle remained.

Bolan pulled a field tourniquet from a split pocket, dropped to one knee, and twisted it quickly and expertly around the terrorist's leg just above the ankle. The plan called for Harker to be hurting by the time he called his meeting to order, not for him to bleed to death beforehand.

The light in the back room came from a lamp with the kind of dim red bulb used in photographers' darkrooms. Jill Breton lay back on a bed in one corner. She was naked, legs splayed at an awkward angle, one arm dangling over the edge of the bed. She stared at her new visitor through dilated eyeballs.

Bolan pulled her gently upright. Her eyes halffocused. Fear came into them as she took in the night man's black-clad image. He tensed, ready to clap a hand over her mouth if she started any noise. Her expression stayed slack.

She offered no protest as Bolan slung her easily over his left shoulder, her body limp, useless, her deadweight requiring Bolan only to check his balance. He maintained his right hand free.

Suddenly she was trying to wrench away, her new-found strength augmented by drugged terror. In fact, Jill Breton was opening her mouth to draw in enough breath to launch a scream that could be heard in Algiers.

Bolan brought her off his shoulder fast and hit her with his fist as he did so, just above the jaw in front of the temple. She folded into his arms, her long blond hair trailing across his face as her nude body slumped against him.

Less than eighty seconds had passed since Bolan first stormed into the billet. He moved back past the dead guards. With his free hand he flicked off the garish yellow light to avoid a silhouette, then carried his shapely burden through the front door. He dumped the girl in the back of Harker's jeep and covered her with a tarp.

From the lightweight backpack, Bolan donned a nylon-shell Windbreaker cut loosely enough to conceal the Ingram still hanging from his neck. He added his "Stone" sunglasses. In the dark, with the lower part of his body hidden by the vehicle, the disguise would have to pass.

Bolan punched the ignition and eased the open rig around Harker's headquarters and turned left toward the front gate. Many of the visiting terrorists were lingering in front of their billets. He avoided all eye contact as he drove.

The guard at the gate was built like a house, about six and a half feet tall and easily three hundred pounds, none of it fat. He had an incongruously small head and a pockmarked face.

"Open up, will you, guy?" Bolan called amiably.

The bear got his bulk through the gatehouse door and came around to the driver's side of the vehicle. When he leaned his weight on it, the whole rig tilted down.

"You're the fella was around already today," the big guard said. "I seen you."

"That's right."

"I thought you was gone."

"Gone where?" The numbers were falling now like a row of dominoes. "Where's there to go around here?"

The big guy squinted, frowned; somewhere in his mind a thought was running around, eluding his grasp. "That's the Chief's jeep."

"Right," Bolan said, grinning to take the edge off the rest of it. "And it's going to be your butt if you don't open the gate. Harker's orders."

Indecision continued to crease the hardguy's unpleasant features. Bolan's right hand tracked for the Beretta. Bolan had come in soft, but if he were going to get the girl to safety he would have to go out hard.

The guy should never have tried to think and move

at the same time. Bolan's good right hand was already on the Beretta.

He shot the monster in the face.

Even though a hunk of the back of the man's head was suddenly missing, he took a step forward and locked hands around Bolan's throat...as though he did not much miss his foreshortened brain.

Bolan got the silencer casing of the pistol under the guy's chin and triggered two rounds. There was the acrid smell of powder-burned flesh as the top of the guy's head went off like his brains had been mined. Lifeless hands dropped away from the Executioner.

There was another shot, nearer and directed at Bolan. He jammed the gearshift lever into low-low and floored the rig. As the front bumper hit the middle of the gate, a further shot from behind shattered the windshield.

The Rover hesitated momentarily as it struck the metal of the two-part gate. Where a chain locked the two parts together in the middle of the rocky roadway, the pale green Land Rover hit with resounding force. Bolan's driving hurled the vehicle through the gate with the thrust of a launch, and then night embraced the rig.

Behind Bolan the camp was in fevered pandemonium. The searchlights mounted on the guard towers bloomed on and swept the compound. Shouts of men in several languages mixed with the *lingua franca* of automatic weapons fire.

Bolan grinned sourly. Luke Harker's ruling house of international terrorism was a house of cards.

Now that he had the girl, the Executioner was going to stick around to knock it over.

13

Mack Bolan's hands, molded minutes before to the shape of gunmetal, now moved sensitively over the unconscious girl in the back of the Rover.

The disheveled blond hair, the smear of blood and dirt across one cheek, the purpling bruises—these superficial, only temporary flaws could not disguise the innate beauty of her high cheekbones, delicate even features, her lips.

Bolan placed his palm flat on her chest, felt the strong heartbeat and the regular rise and fall of her breathing. There was nothing wrong with her that time wouldn't heal.

Nothing physical, anyway. The psychological scars left by Luke Harker might in fact never disappear.

Mack Bolan held no rancor for the girl. On the contrary, in certain ways he both sympathized with and admired her. Sure, hooking up with Harker was wrongheaded, but dropping out of college and her aimless travels were part of a quest for someone important, maybe a substitute for the father she never had. That, along with her earlier commitment to social causes, had made her easy prey for a creep like

Harker, an emotional parasite who could sense her need and pretend to respond to it. Jill Breton's own yearnings blinded her to Harker's vicious self-interest.

Misguided though she might be, she was also independent and strong-minded. Bolan had seen her spirit in the camp, though negatively displayed. His fine-tuned ability to sense a person's true qualities told him that this one was essentially a good woman. Defeated, as was her father, in familial love, her frustration and anger warped her true personality. Just as her father had nearly made a mistake that put a nuclear device in terrorist hands, so had she made the mistake of putting her own safety in those grasping paws.

It had been a harsh lesson for both father and daughter. But maybe, Mack hoped, they would learn from it, learn to express the feelings for each other that had always lain dormant within them.

Jill moaned and stirred, then opened her eyes. She stared up at the big man hovering over her. Night had fully fallen by now, but the sky was peppered with stars and the desertscape was bright as twilight.

Her eyes opened wider. "You're one of them. You were down there, you're the man in the shades." Her tone was rational, if fear-tinged. Whatever she had been high on had been knocked out of her.

"How do you feel?"

"How the hell do you think I feel?" She sat up and the sheet slipped to her waist. She snatched it to her to cover her breasts. "I've got a headache. You think I'm some kind of junkie or something?" She looked at him bitterly. "You're one of them. You were in Algiers." She leaned back in exhausted resignation. "I know what you want—the same as Harker. He said he loved me, that we were going to work together to do things that would really help people. . ."

The girl began to sob. At first quietly, then more openly. Bolan did not interrupt. He went to the Rover and dug into one of the flight bags.

He came back and tossed a shirt and a pair of belted slacks into the girl's lap. She turned to him uncertainly. Bolan caught a glimpse of her sleek white nakedness in the starlight as she replaced the sheet with the clothing while he lit a cigarette and stood smoking in the cooling darkness.

She teetered a moment on unsteady legs, then made herself stand upright, free of the vehicle's support. Even in her pain and confusion she had made herself look damned good. The too-long legs of the slacks were rolled up to mid-calf, the tails of the man-tailored shirt were tied beneath her breasts, leaving a wide expanse of flat bare midriff. She ran fingers through her tangled blond hair.

Bolan went to the Rover and removed the shattered windshield from its hinged mounts across the hood. He cast the useless screen into a shallow gulley.

Then he reached for the munitions bag. He pulled out the Ingram, substituted the clip with a full one, and began to replace the nine expended rounds in the other magazine. The girl watched unsteadily, but with curiosity.

"You're not one of them after all, are you?"

"No more than you are," the big man said. "Do you realize that Luke Harker was trying to trade you for a new kind of nuclear weapon that your father's company invented?"

"My father—" Jill began in a hateful tone edged with contempt.

"Go easy, lady," Bolan cut her off. "When I'm done you can tell me all about your father, if you still want to."

Jill shrugged and leaned back against the Land Rover.

"No matter what your father did—and he did plenty, Jill, for you—Luke Harker was going to kill you. If Harker did get the bomb, he was going to replicate it and sell copies to any crackpot gang of sloganeering gun-creeps who could pay the freight. People like the ones in that camp right now."

Bolan finished checking out the M-10 and turned the cocking handle to set the safety. Then he gave his attention to a quick field-strip of the Beretta.

"They were going to use those bombs to kill people," Bolan went on purposefully. "Not their own kind. Not soldiers. Innocent people, people who had the bad luck to be in the wrong place at the wrong time. People like you."

Bolan's fingers flew over the Beretta, reassembling the autopistol. He seated a fresh clip and chambered a round and sheathed the weapon in its accustomed spot.

"If you think your father is the killer and those men the heroes, you'd better think again. Sure, your father makes weapons, but not to start wars. They exist to stop egomaniacs like Luke Harker from turning the world into their own bloody little playground."

Bolan looked up from his work. The girl was able to meet his gaze only for a moment before turning away.

"There's one more thing you should know about your father," Bolan pressed. "Yesterday he went up against five of those people singlehandedly. He risked his life because he thought he could save yours."

Jill began to cry again. Bolan went to her, put his big hands on her shoulders.

"He loves you, Jill," the man in black said quietly.

"All I wanted was to make the world a better place," the girl murmured.

"So do I, lady," Bolan said.

"I'm sorry. And you saved my life."

Bolan nodded his acceptance of her words. "But it's not over yet," he said.

In a larger sense Mack Bolan knew it would never be over. This was war everlasting.

To the Executioner the phenomenon of international terrorism was like the Hydra, the many-headed monster in Greek mythology. Each time one of its heads was cut off, two new ones grew in its place.

Yet eventually the beast was slain by Hercules.

Bolan was no moralist, no politician, no narrow-visioned superpatriot. He was simply a man who believed in the American system, and who was willing to back that conviction with action.

His researches on the subject had convinced him that democracy was the best system that Man in all the millenia of human existence had devised for the orderly governance of free men and women.

As he knew it, it was a system of rights—to speak one's mind, to be secure in the privacy of one's home, to face one's accuser and be tried by one's peers, to bear arms and defend oneself.

It was also a system of responsibilities, in which all people for the sake of their own opportunities and destiny had to respect the rights of all the others, in which no man could be allowed to abrogate those cherished privileges that democracy granted. The most sacred trust of every American for over two hundred years was to protect that system against those who would pervert or usurp any part of it.

The threat against which Mack Bolan was constantly pitting his warrior skills wanted to do just that.

International terrorism was not a bunch of groups with strange names or initials knocking people off in foreign countries that most people could not pinpoint on a world map.

International terrorism had grown more sophisticated. That's why the reviving Mafia liked it so much. That's why Russia liked it so much.

And terrorism's primary target, the one big objective of its concerted thrust, has always been the United States of America.

Not long before this night, Bolan had sat in the War Room at Stony Man Farm in West Virginia, in front of a video display terminal as Aaron "the Bear" Kurtzman called up the latest facts and figures:

Fact: In nearly two out of five incidents of international terrorism, U.S. citizens or property are the primary targets.

Fact: In a recent year, an average of one American was under attack by terrorists somewhere in the world every day.

Fact: In that same year terrorists murdered ten Americans and injured ninety-four others.

Fact: In that period not a single major terrorist attack was directed against Russia, its satellites, or any of its so-called "client" states.

Fact: A Soviet defector who had worked for several years in the KGB's Department VIII, which comprised the Mediterranean area including the Middle East and the Arab nations of northern Africa, delivered documents which showed direct Department VIII assistance to ultra-left terrorist activities against pro-Western governments. The KGB was committed to (1) operations sabotaging Saudi Arabian oilfields;

(2) the promotion of terrorism in other Arab oil suppliers to the U.S.; and (3) abetting what the documents called "a brutal campaign of terror, kidnapping, and assassination" in the crucially situated nation of Turkey.

Fact: The USSR and the Libyan leader Muammar Khaddafi struck the biggest arms deal in history: a $12 billion order for Russian armament, equivalent to over one-half million dollars worth of weapons for each of Khaddafi's 22,000 army troops. Except, of course, most of it is destined for transshipment to pro-Soviet leftists throughout the world. Fact after chilling fact.

Soviet backing for the terrorist movement has included tanks, fighter planes, naval craft, and missiles. It also involves financial support, sophisticated training, and established escape routes and sanctuaries. But the most important contribution has been the organization necessary for *inter-terrorist* cooperation.

Instance: In 1966 Fidel Castro played host to the so-called "Tricontinental Congress" in Cuba's capital of Havana. More than five hundred delegates attended what was ostensibly a peaceful convocation of Third World nations; in fact it was a call to arms. One resolution emphasized the need for "close cooperation between Socialist countries and national liberation movements," a clear indication of the Soviet-terrorist link. Another resolution stated the summit delegates' purpose: "to devise a global revolutionary strategy to counter the global strategy of American imperialism.'' It was no less than a call for underground and undeclared warfare against the United States.

Instance: In October of 1971 the Italian leftist publisher Giangiacomo Feltrinelli, a committed terrorist who would later blow himself up while sabotaging a power line, organized a terrorist convocation at a Jesuit college in Florence. The purpose was to launch the Red International, a leftist coalition. Attendees included the IRA, the Red Brigades, the Basque ETA, the Argentinian ERP, the American Black Panthers, and of course the Palestinians.

Instance: In May, 1972 PFLP leader Dr. George Habash convened an avowed terrorist summit in Baddawi, Lebanon, where twelve terrorist groups signed a ''Declaration of Support'' for the Provisional terrorist wing of the IRA, paving the way for international underground support of that group. Cuba offered training in terror and guerrilla warfare. Khaddafi of Libya provided armament. Both offers were gratefully accepted.

Any man other than Mack Bolan might have been overwhelmed by the extent of such hellish enmity.

But this was the Executioner's kind of fight, the fight to which he had dedicated his life. Wherever he found the spoor of terrorism, he found too the trace of people he had met before, the types of rat he had been busy obliterating despite the fabric of legitimate business and politics they hid behind. Large-scale organization was no problem to the Executioner. The obliteration would continue as long as the vermin were identifiable.

However much they cloaked their filth in the mumbo-jumbo rhetoric of humanism and liberation, the terrorists, like the organized criminals, were in his sights and he would not falter.

They were all the same, that type. Despite fancy connections, and all the fancy legwork that went with them, they were still the kind to use a one-quarter-inch electric drill on some innocent victim's kneecap. Nasty, whichever way you looked at it.

How will the vermin feel when their horrors fall back on them, when, through Bolan's will, the winds of war shift direction and the poisons descend upon their own heads? When the dry desert wind changes and the firestorm swallows them up?

Bolan would give them all a chance to find out.

He stood on the bluff and stared into the distance at Harker's compound. The searchlights had turned night into day. Men were hustling across the grounds, their shouts carrying eerily on the thin desert air. Bolan spotted Richard Wolfe. Harker was not visible.

Tex Hoffman was leaning against the captured Rover. "It's coming down," he said when Bolan approached. It was not a question.

Bolan nodded. "If Harker lives," the big guy said,

"you know that you die. He'll find you wherever you go."

Now the other man nodded, his Stetson almost mimicking the movement.

"If he dies," Bolan continued, "you still have me to reckon with. If you ever get involved with any of those people again, I'll know about it. If you even think about returning to the wrong side, it'll be the last thought you have."

"Thanks, man," Tex said. "Sounds real appealing."

"I owe you nothing, Hoffman. I'm giving you a better deal than you deserve. And I want something from you in return."

"What's that?"

"You give me exactly forty minutes," Bolan said. "I mean forty, not ten seconds more. Mark when I start out from here. If I'm not back when the time is up, you take the girl and the Rover—there's gas in the back. You deliver the girl to the American Embassy in Algiers and you disappear. You don't go in with her and you don't say anything to anyone. Questions?"

The other guy shook his head.

"Your word," Bolan demanded.

"You got it, man."

Bolan was at the edge of the bluff and starting down when he heard Tex call after him. He paused and turned.

"Hey man," the guy said. His voice broke slightly. "Good luck."

Yeah, good luck. Good luck and a steady hand and the experience of the many battles that had come before this one. All of that might bring him once more through the firestorm.

Had to and would.

There would be other battlegrounds calling soon enough.

14

Richard Wolfe was no stranger to violence. He was not a rich man's pup like Luke Harker, but a product of the streets of the Flatbush section of Brooklyn. He grew up with violence in a fifth-story three-room walk-up that made do for his mother, father, and two older sisters. Although he could not remember it, he knew the very first sounds he heard were fists striking flesh, the ragged cries of pain and rage.

His father was an ironworker and he had made good money—when he was sober enough to work. Then the routine was always the same: Dick Wolfe Senior would go to work at six in the morning, hit the nearest bar at three in the afternoon, stagger in at nine at night, drunk and mean. Usually it was Wolfe's mother who got beat on, but occasionally the old man turned on the kids.

One occasion stood out in Wolfe's mind. He was nine years old when it happened. His older sister Angie had turned sixteen that day, and with the money that their mother gave her she bought a new sweater. She was just back from the store and modeling it for them when the old man walked in, stinking drunk as always.

He took one look at Angie and started screaming at her. She was a filthy little whore just like her mother, he yelled.

Angie knew what was coming and ran into the girls' bedroom, the old man right behind her. For some reason Wolfe followed.

As he watched from the doorway, his father stalked across the room, grabbed the front of Angie's sweater in one big calloused mitt, and ripped it clean off her. She wasn't wearing anything underneath, and as she stood there with nothing on except a pair of shorts, the damnedest look came over the old man's face.

Then the old man saw Wolfe standing in the doorway and the look changed instantly to anger. He crossed the little room in two steps and that was the last thing Wolfe remembered until he woke up in the hospital. His left arm was broken in two places and his body was a mass of welts and bruises. For a week afterward he pissed blood.

The cast came off after nine weeks. Three days later Wolfe stole twenty bucks from the old man's wallet while he was passed out in front of the TV and he bought a nickel-plated .22 revolver from an older guy with buck teeth who hung around the Nedick's on the corner. He spent the rest of the afternoon on the roof of the apartment building, sighting down the barrel at pigeons and trying to figure out the best place to kill his old man.

Before he came up with a place to bushwack him that wouldn't get the family involved, his old man saved him the trouble. He showed up at work one morning at six with the better part of a pint of Jim Beam in him. Minutes later he stepped off a cross-piece and fell twenty-seven stories, bouncing off a scaffolding at the eleventh floor. He ended up on his back on a piece of pre-formed concrete, six feet of reinforcement sticking out of his chest.

Wolfe was disappointed that he didn't get to do the job himself. But he figured that at least his old lady would be happy. Instead, she went straight to pieces right after the funeral. For weeks she kept collapsing in tears for no reason. Then she took to the bottle so hard it made the old man look like a temperance worker.

Wolfe Sr. had been dead less than a year when Wolfe came home one day and found his old lady facedown on the floor in a mess of her own puke. The police coroner listed cause of death as "acute ethanol poisoning" and the M.E.'s autopsy report stated that she had consumed at least two quarts of vodka in the four hours prior to death.

Angie did her best to take care of him and his other sister Miriam, two years younger than Angie. Miriam was always real wild, staying out all night, getting arrested for shoplifting or joyriding, even skin-popping heroin, while Angie did her best to be a mother to both of the younger kids. That's why it always struck Wolfe funny how they turned out. Miriam, the wild one, was married to a shoe salesman over in Queens. And Angie was working in a place that called itself a "massage parlor" near Times Square. That was a while back, of course. Wolfe hadn't heard from either of them for nearly ten years.

Because he was always overweight the other kids on the street gave Wolfe shit. That ended right after the old man was killed, when Wolfe used the .22 to shatter the right ankle of an older kid who tried to shake him down for pocket change. And there was no one answerable for Richard Wolfe. Thus he began to command a new respect in the neighborhood. By the time he was fourteen he had his own gang. He had learned to use his muscle, and to be discreet about it.

Wolfe got into Columbia University by breaking into the office of the high school he had sporadically attended, stealing the records of the class valedictorian, and doctoring them so they appeared to be his own. At first he paid his way through college by holding up liquor stores and mugging people near the theater district. Later he worked an in with a guy named Passerrelli whose brother worked for an up-and-coming Mafia mobster named Augie Marinello. Passerrelli got Wolfe a job stealing expensive foreign cars to order.

It was during that period that Wolfe hooked up with Luke Harker.

Then the violence—the cop they killed, the bank job—became a way to attract attention, to make a reputation.

When they got to Europe their reputation came along for the ride.

And Richard Wolfe's talents came to full flower.

The years on the Brooklyn streets coupled with the burst of urban terrorism of the protest days had made him a cool hand in any dangerous situation. The college education—he had concentrated on psychology, world history, political science, and he did well—coupled with the practical experience of manipulating people against the Vietnam War made him a savvy strategist. He could meet the terrorists on their own ground and keep Harker on the path to success at the same time.

Harker was the public figure, the one with the satanic style when he delivered a speech. He was the one with an almost mystic power over people, the hypnotic ability to sway and influence opinion and action. But he never could have succeeded without Wolfe, who arranged the connections, made sure they cozied up to the right people, got them out when the getting was good.

Wolfe was a master of the situational response. He could think on his feet, and he knew instinctively what to do under any given set of circumstances.

Except that he had never seen this kind of situation.

Jon Carter, the urbane Mafia Black Ace, was equally concerned but for different reasons.

He stood up, dusted his hands together briskly, and said, "Is he the last one?"

"Yes," Richard Wolfe confirmed.

In death the monster looked somehow smaller, his huge bulk shrivelled up as the life blood had run out of the hole in him. Carter grimaced in distaste.

"Are you sure?"

"I'm sure."

"I'm glad to hear that," Carter said sarcastically. "He was one of ours, you know." He had been leery of this whole business from the moment Contadina had been contacted and invited. Carter had checked out Harker, didn't very much like what he had learned. But Contadina had insisted that too many other groups had already accepted. They must attend to protect their own interests. Carter had agreed with great reservation.

He had not, however, expected things to fuck up this badly. If any more shit came down, Carter was personally going to tear Harker's arms and legs off, and he wanted Wolfe to know it.

"Who were the others?"

Wolfe returned Carter's gaze. He was a cool customer, Carter had to give him that. This whole deal is coming down around his ears, plus his boss has just been shot in the foot by some unknown force and Wolfe is still trying to get it together.

"One of the IRA Provos," Wolfe said. "The Latino was with the MIR, the Chilean group. The Jap was Masaki Asada."

"Is that supposed to mean something to me?" Carter said.

Ricardo Roybal materialized out of the shadows between the two billets. "He was the Operational Director for the Red Army's European cell. He was heading their delegation."

Carter laughed humorlessly.

Wolfe stiffened. He turned on his heel and walked away across the compound.

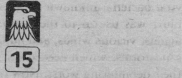

15

The cross hairs of the infrared sniperscope were centered on Luke Harker's chest. The upper part of the round frame revealed the terrorist "field marshal's" face. The deep V of the man's eyebrows was furrowed with pain and anger, and his mouth was set in a straight hard line. The scope swept the length of his lanky body to reveal his right foot, swathed in white bandages stained dark red in the middle.

Mack Bolan grinned. By this time Harker's foot would be throbbing unmercifully. Not only would the constant pain make it hard for him to think clearly, but it would also serve as a nagging reminder that he had been attacked in his own billet on his own compound.

Bolan's vantage point was a little more than halfway down the bluff where he had set up his own base. A small streambed cut down the steep slope, the relic of a time thousands of years earlier when the Sahara was not a desert but a semi-tropical region capable of supporting vegetation of all sorts. There was no water now, of course. At the compound it had been trucked in, and was probably stored in below-ground containers, and fluoridated against viral bacteria unknown in other continents. The arid bluff was useful to the camp. It was a protection against vicious winds, and nullified the possibility of sandstorms, which needed flat dunes to get going at their debilitating worst. Now the bluff was useful to Bolan.

His position was about two hundred meters from the front gate of the compound. That put him roughly two hundred and seventy-five meters from each corner, where the big searchlights were mounted on gimbals. A uniformed man was stationed on each guard tower.

One of the men was sweeping his light back and forth within the grounds, illuminating the milling groups of armed men.

The man in the tower on the left stood ready to sweep the compound too—with a 7.62x54mm tripod-mounted Kalashnikov PKMS heavy machine gun.

Yeah, Luke Harker would be having intimations of mortality round about now. Intimations that his whole grand plan could turn on him. He was apparently willing to open fire on his own guests if he had to. Yeah.

It wasn't too bad an idea, but it didn't quite fit the Executioner's plan.

Bolan chambered a massive 500-grain round into a Weatherby Mark V rifle. The weapon had been stashed with Bolan's gear in the useful Rover. In his hands the big rifle became a lethal messenger of long-distance death. The .460 Magnum slug left the 26-inch barrel at 2700 feet per second, at an incredible muzzle energy of over *8000* foot-pounds. At 100 yards the mid-range trajectory was a respectable .7 inches; that increased to 10 inches at 300 yards, but Bolan's experience with the big gun was so extensive that computing the correction factor had become an automatic part of aiming.

Bolan rested the Weatherby on the edge of the trench and sighted on the tower on his right. He'd get these two first, then he'd go for the two similar searchlight towers at the rear. He waited until the guard had swung the big light in the opposite direction from him, then pressed his right eye against the soft rubber housing of the scope, settling the cross hairs at a point eight inches above the center of the light's housing. Then he triggered the round.

The searchlight exploded in a shower of sparks and glass. Immediately Bolan tracked the Mark V ninety degrees to his left, sighted on the second tower, sent another high velocity round through the guts of the fixed searchlight there.

The machine gunner spotted Bolan's muzzle flash. He spun the belt-fed PKMS around and sprayed endless lead toward Bolan's position.

Except that the man who had triggered the flash was already forty meters from that first position and was closing in on the compound.

Bolan cut to his left, moving invisibly through the semidarkness he had just created. As he reached the tower the gunner was feeding the end of a new link-belt magazine into the PKMS.

Bolan rolled a grenade under the tower as he dog-trotted by. Behind him the chattergun started up its stutter for a split second, then was swallowed up in the roar of the grenade that turned the tower into a wrenching heap of scrap metal.

Men started hollering in several languages. Bolan saw the shadowy, blurred forms of a group of Harker's TWPLF troops streaming toward the two remaining towers at the compound's rear.

The man in black dropped to one knee and brought up the Weatherby. It was not the ideal firing posture but he had cut the range to less than fifty meters. The Magnum slug reached the searchlight with perfect accuracy. The shattering noise was noisy but brief.

Bolan saw that two guards who had been manning the third tower were in the process of bailing out.

The decision was a little tardy. They were halfway down the ladder when Bolan's grenade lofted in under them.

One of them tried to go up, the other tried to go down, and they were clawing at each other when the blast ended the argument for good.

As Bolan hit the last leg of his circumnavigation of the fence-line, an amplified voice sounded above the echoes of the blast.

"Your attention please." It was Richard Wolfe, talking over the p.a. system. His voice was actually calm and controlled.

"We are under attack from an outside force, repeat, an *outside* force." A force, yeah, of one. "For your own safety all delegates are requested to go immediately to the meeting hall. There is no longer any danger. The soldiers of the Third World People's Liberation Front have already repelled the attack."

Hate to disappoint you, guy, and Bolan rolled a grenade under the last of the four towers. A moment later the hollow boom of the explosion, followed immediately by the tearing of metal and the full screams of wounded men, combined to drown out Wolfe's words.

Another voice started up, repeating the orders in Spanish. Slowly the tide of milling, half-panicked men appeared to start moving toward the big building near the compound's center. Bolan spotted Frank Contadina at one edge of the surging crowd. On one of his flanks was Jon Carter, a Uzi submachine gun in one hand and Contadina's elbow in the other.

Rikki the Hyena was on Contadina's other side. There was a strangely tranquil and beatific look of bliss on his soft features. From Bolan's distance he looked like a kid at a fireworks display. The sudden violence all around him had brought the first touch of emotion to his features. Rikki was playfully sweeping the space before him with a Skorpion machine pistol, as if he were looking for something, anything, that he could shoot.

Richard Wolfe had reached the double doorway of the big structure. He held the bullhorn in one hand

and beckoned with the other. Apparently the guy's experience with mob psychology was paying off. Given no other instructions, confused and shaken after explosives had ripped out of nowhere, the crowd was willing to follow any suggestion for action, if it was given with authority. In a few minutes the body of men was inside.

Which was fine with the "attacking force" watching from the shadows. Mack Bolan had intended that Luke Harker's big summit conference take place as scheduled.

As scheduled, yeah.

But not quite as planned.

The Executioner had a few changes to make in the agenda.

16

"Could I have your attention, please. Please, your attention."

Richard Wolfe was sweating like a pig. He was mopping at his forehead constantly with a handkerchief that was already soaked. His shirt clung to him like a clammy second skin, and he could feel his heart pounding. There was a tightness across his chest. Despite all of this he was managing to project an outward appearance of calm. His voice, he was pleased to note, was firm and steady.

"We have determined without a doubt that the attacks on this base have come from outside." As far as Wolfe could tell, that was true, although he had no idea what it meant. For all he knew there were people in the hall at that moment who were behind the attack. The important thing was to sound positive, definite.

Eventually there were over two hundred people in the hall. Despite the air conditioning and the fans suspended from the ceiling it was hot and stuffy in the huge quonset hut and the air was rapidly becoming foul with the smell of cigarettes and rancid sweat.

About forty of those present were Harker's TWPLF gunmen. At least eight of the force had been killed in the slug and grenade blitz that took out the guard towers. Wolfe had brought the rest inside quite deliberately: he didn't want to lose any more to ambushes or sniper attacks.

The rest of the men present were from the delegations.

And every man in the room was armed.

"You know of the killings that have taken place," Wolfe went on, "of the deaths of our brothers from Japan, Chile, Northern Ireland, and—" he glanced at Frank Contadina. Shit, what were you supposed to call those guys? "—the group from the United States," he finished. "We now know that those killings were a deliberate act of provocation, an attempt to turn us against one another, to put brother at the throat of brother. No man in this room had anything to do with it."

He hoped they bought it. He was fully aware of the suspicious mutterings and looks directed his way. The microphone was mounted on a raised platform at one end of the airless building. The delegates had formed little knots below and in front of him, all of them staying pretty much to themselves and giving wide berths to their neighbors.

Wolfe looked around for Rikki the Hyena. He was not with Carter and Contadina, who had staked out a spot against the wall nearby. Then Wolfe saw Rikki standing at the very back of the hall, his dark blank eyes taking in the room, a chilling look of anticipation on his face, like a strangely ungrown person.

"Even more than before," Wolfe went on, "the need for us all to band together, to work in concert for the same noble ends, is vital. This attack has failed because together we are too strong. We must remain together and grow even stronger."

Wolfe hoped *to hell* they bought it.

"I have been informed that Field Marshal Harker has just left his billet," Wolfe wrapped up, "now that the attack has been repulsed and his safety, like ours, has been assured. He will be arriving to open the meeting momentarily."

Why not just crawl right out on another limb? In fact Richard Wolfe had not seen Luke Harker since the first grenade went off. He was too busy heading off a full-scale riot.

If the guy didn't show up soon there was going to be another one. And Wolfe knew that this time it would roll right over him.

The murmuring in the room grew louder. He looked around and saw too many pairs of eyes staring at him. He felt naked, very vulnerable.

He was relieved to get his feet off the raised platform and back down on the hut's concrete floor—until a hand locked around his upper arm.

It was Jon Carter.

"Keep cool," Carter said, so quietly that Wolfe could barely hear him. "Any ruckus and this place is going to go off like Chinese New Year."

Wolfe let himself be pulled along by Carter.

They found Frank Contadina scared witless. He was pushed back against the wall like a cornered animal, and he was sweating worse than Wolfe.

"What are you and Harker trying to pull, you son of a bitch?" Contadina hissed. The urbane and unruffled international businessman was gone. To Contadina, violence was always something you told one of your boys to do to someone else.

"What are you talking about?" Wolfe snapped.

"That big dark bastard, that Stone—he's working for you."

"Bullshit."

"Sure he is," Contadina pushed. "You're trying to take over the whole ball game, you and Harker. The meet here was a setup. You get us all together so Stone and those gun-punks you call soldiers can go to work on us."

"Frank," Carter said soothingly.

"You're crazy, Contadina," Wolfe put in.

The old man's face purpled with rage. A guy could sign his own death warrant by saying far less to Frank Contadina.

"For all I know Stone is *your* man," Wolfe spat back. "He looked to me like the kind of cheap flashy hood you'd be likely to keep around." He snapped a hard look at Carter and was gratified by the cold anger on the man's face. "Why the hell would Harker attack his own base? Let me put it to you this way—if Stone *is* your boy, you're making the biggest mistake of your life—what's left of it.''

Richard Wolfe did not particularly fear dying. It was all a matter of timing. Ideally he would like to know from what direction death was coming and who was bringing it. Right now the timing was in favor of his life. He was spared by the arrival of his boss.

Luke Harker had slipped completely loose from his moorings.

Wolfe realized it the moment the guy walked into the hall. His cap was missing and his hair was tangled and uncombed and slick with sweat. His shirt was soaked dark under either arm and half-buttoned. The wound in his right foot must have reopened. The once-white bandage was now soaked red. Behind him Harker left a line of greasy crimson footprints.

The room went deadly quiet. Every eye in the place landed on this would-be *capo di tutti capi*. Wolfe scanned the faces and he could see it in them. They knew. They were aware that Harker had flipped off his rocker and landed on his head.

Wolfe had to do something, get the guy out of there, anything. But to where? And then what? If Harker had been difficult to control before, now it would be impossible. And Wolfe had his own ass to cover.

He stood there staring at the guy, mesmerized like everyone else in the hall by the manic image Harker presented.

Groups parted to let Harker pass. Harker paid no attention to anyone on either side of him. His eyes, the pupils dilated and the whites bloodshot, were stabbing into Wolfe.

"She's gone," Harker said. He was speaking to Wolfe and his voice was not loud, but his tone was crazy and strong and vibrant and reached every corner of the hall. It was his public voice, the voice meant to be heard, the voice that for years had swayed and captivated people and made them do Luke Harker's bidding.

"Luke . . ." Wolfe began.

"I've been all over the compound, looked everywhere. She's gone. What do you think of that?"

"Take it easy."

Harker swayed backward, caught himself, leaned toward Wolfe.

"You took her," he hissed.

Wolfe approached and put his hand on the other man's arm. Harker slapped it away. "Oh, I know it was that big son of a bitch in black who took her. I'm not crazy. But he was working for you all along, wasn't he? You wanted it all, right?"

Still nobody moved. Wolfe's mind raced, searching desperately for a way to defuse this situation before it was too late.

"Where is that big bastard?" Harker demanded.

"Right here, Harker."

And then the big guy in the aviator shades was standing right there with him.

And Richard Wolfe knew that "too late" had just arrived.

17

On the other side of the hall someone coughed. But no one moved.

"What the fuck is going on here?" Stone demanded. His eyes blazed at each of the four men—Carter, Contadina, Wolfe, and finally Harker. He pinned each for a crucial moment with his gaze. The plan was on the heartbeat and Bolan's every gesture, expression, and nuance of movement had to be critical, perfect.

"Maybe you're the one who ought to—" Wolfe began.

"Shove it." The big man in the shades cut him off.

Bolan's back was to the rest of the room now. He opened the nylon-shell Windbreaker enough to let the four of them see the big silver .44 AutoMag strapped to his waist.

But not enough to let them see the silenced Beretta slung under his left arm.

"You, Contadina," Bolan snapped, picking the weakest link. "What's happening here?"

"I'll tell you what's happening." It was Luke Harker who spoke. "You took my girl. I want her back."

Bolan was down to the single numbers now. This man was jealous crazy.

"You ought to know, Harker," he said, still only loud enough for the other three to hear.

"What you talking about?"

"You killed her, Luke." Before anyone could chew on that, Bolan turned to the hall. "This man has killed his hostage. He realized he'd fucked up, that the U.S. was going to come down on him if they had to chase him forever. So the heat is on Harker—" Bolan raised his voice "—and on everyone else here too. They figure you are all involved."

Bolan turned his icy gaze back on Harker. "Luke here made up all that crap about the 'big bastard in black.' He was even nuts enough to shoot himself in the foot—just look at him..."

"That's a lie," Harker screamed maniacally, his voice booming across the room as his brain struggled against the trap that had closed on it.

His hand snaked for the automatic on his hip.

But the AutoMag was already in Bolan's fist.

The oversized handgun thundered and bucked.

Something impossible happened to Luke Harker's face.

The V of his eyebrows seemed to dip toward his nose, and then the nose altogether caved in and took those eyebrows with it and all became lost in the collapsing structure of the front of his skull. The 240-grain brain-shredder erupted out of the back of his head. A frothy fountain of flesh and teeth and bone and gray matter was evident as his body lifted off the floor. Harker slammed backward; what was left above the shoulders was not, finally, anything human.

For a dreadful second no one moved. Bolan did a quick scan of the room, his senses on full combat alert, his battle instincts alive from the tension-waves coursing through the place.

A would-be hero on the other side of the hall, in the uniform of Harker's TWPLF, brought up his AK-47.

Simultaneously Bolan brought up his AutoMag. From his firing-range stance he dispatched a Magnum messenger to the guy's gut.

And the meeting hall erupted.

Two men started shooting at each other. Then a third, an Armenian, aimed his automatic at the Turk who was settling his own score and his target shimmied as if some kid had been taking potshots at a bag full of rats. Lead tore ragged holes in human flesh.

The hall filled with sights of obscenity, of gross subhumanity. Bolan eyeballed the scene and took real care. All about was the enraged bellowing of trained killers held in bay for too long, their blood-lust now suddenly unleashed.

He saw four men, less than fifteen feet away, fighting clear of metal chairs and a table as they lunged to safety. But too late. Some unnamed terrorist's Remington 1100 Magnum autoloader was pumping into their vicinity and they were each intercepting its issue. One got it in the lower left mouth, his yells of confusion and aggression becoming one swallowed grunt of shock in a shredded throat. The other three took theirs in the bowels; clean in, very dirty out.

The fight was everything now, and everywhere. The hall was host to a mindless unleashing of all those lethal grains of hate that had been coursing through these hoodlums' veins like an African nation in revolt. The crack of what sounded like an Enforcer 45 acp added to the cacophony of the building, bringing a taste of the military to this anonymous hole, this boxed afterbirth of hell for the denizens of nowhere to eat.

Bolan spared a split second to realize how far this crazed reality was from the concerns of Harrison Breton and his wayward daughter Jill. *This* was madness incarnate. *That* was at least hope, the biological light of life, a flicker of familial caring. He wanted to shoot gut now, bust bone. His hair hurt with the need to slice a skull in this place and sluice the vacuous innards of a terrorist's brainpan down into the dusty gutter of Algeria and thence, immediately, inevitably, to the smoking underworld, that bad neighborhood from whence those stinking non-brains had surely once come.

Bolan was on the hot verge of sending fire lacing into the environ. Then he saw Contadina edging along the near wall, followed by Carter. So...despite the imploding carnage of this game, Aces were still high, huh?

There was neither time nor purpose here to find meat with swift steel—much as the Executioner's instincts screamed to pop life open and spray ruptured grease on these walls, to find flesh per flash with his military precision, he had other moves to make. Let the other boys take no prisoners. He had a very particular body count to take.

The big room shook with scraping metal and shatterd glass and the resounding screams of Animal Man, damn near an earthquake of perdition. The Remington repeated again. AK-47s hammered dead air. The Enforcer spoke up, was silenced by 240 grains of .44 Magnum. Bolan ducked to the wall.

Frank Contadina clawed desperately at Bolan's arm, his face ashen with terror. Bolan pushed the Mafia boss into Jon Carter, dropped to a half-crouch and cut along the wall toward the door he had marked the moment he had entered.

A swarthy Arab in a burnoose tried to brain him with the butt of his empty rifle. The AutoMag spoke and tore a tunnel through the fedayeen's entrails. The guy flopped away and Bolan caught a split-second image of another Arab behind him using his thumb to plug a geyser of blood that pumped from his jugular where the .44 had gone after passing through his buddy.

Another one of Harker's boys was standing, panic-frozen, at the door. Bolan slammed the barrel of the big handgun down on the crown of the guy's head and heard the crack of skullbone.

At the same moment a finger of fire traced along Bolan's right side, just below the last rib. He was hit.

The AutoMag spoke once more and a ragged-edged hole appeared in the metal door where the bolt had been. Bolan booted the door and it flew back on its hinges and he half-stumbled into the night, the wrenching motion bringing another stab of pain to his side.

No more than ten beats had passed since the Executioner had fired the first shot. Behind him pandemonium raged on. Bullets punched through the corrugated tin above his head.

The nightfighter moved along the wall in a crouch, head low, ripping off the Windbreaker to reveal the turtlenecked blacksuit beneath. His fingers probed at his side, found a rip in the elastic material and beneath it a four-inch groove in his flesh, sticky with blood. Mack Bolan had been hurt worse, but it was a painful distraction; it was messier than what he had taken on his last flash visit to Vietnam.

The M-203 was under a tarp against the side of the meeting hall where he had stashed it. Bolan charged the M-16 autorifle that formed the upper half of the hybrid weapon, thumbed a green-and-gold HE grenade into the M-79 launcher tandemed below. From a slit pocket in the blacksuit came a medicated field compress which he slapped over the bullet crease.

He came around the end of the long building just as the front doors broke open and gunfire burst into the warm night. A dozen of Harker's men came streaming out in ragged formation and headed for the armory double-time.

Bolan waited in the shadows for the five or so beats it took them to cross the open space. The men were shouting at each other and straining at the big sliding door of the munitions storehouse when Bolan's hand moved to the blacksuit's chest pack.

The remote detonator was a black metal box about the size of a pack of cigarettes. It had been designed to Bolan's specifications by engineers attached to the National Security Council. He flipped up a cap at one end that covered a recessed well as big around as a half-dollar, and flipped the toggle switch inside. This armed the transmitter. A panel on one side slid open to reveal a series of four buttons.

Bolan punched the first two simultaneously.

The sliding door came rocketing off its track like a giant fist had slammed into it from inside the building. One of the men who had been tugging at it looked down at the ground in shuddering shock where both of his forearms lay, severed at the elbow as the edge of the door shot by. Other men had been crushed under the door's weight.

Then the secondaries went off. A rolling ball of flame came angrily billowing out of the space where the door had been. None of the men had time to scream. The cleansing fire turned them instantly into smoldering cinders.

It was a deadly chain reaction. The next explosion tore a ragged hole in the tin roof and a pillar of red flame reached a hundred feet into the night sky. Red-hot metal debris rained down onto the dusty, rocky ground.

And then the secondaries began overlapping and for a full fifteen seconds they became one immense roar, the primal sound of high explosive and ripping metal and scorching super-heated fire. What had once been a building was now completely obscured by the inferno. The hungry flames found more to consume in the nearby billets. Several of these burst into a conflagration like the far suburbs of Hiroshima.

Bolan rose out of the shadow, aware of but detached from the pain in his side. He stalked back toward the open door of the meeting hall.

Two terrorist hardmen stood in the doorway. They were staring at the flames like mesmerized moths. One of them spotted the black apparition coming out of the shadows and tried to work his mouth to sputter a warning. Bolan's M-16 made its point first and the guy and his partner flopped back over the threshold into the building.

Bolan stepped over them on his return to the hall.

There he saw a scene of concentrated carnage the likes of which he had rarely seen in all his years of warfare.

The meeting hall was carpeted with bodies, with pieces of bodies. The concrete floor beneath his feet was slick with blood. In some places the corpses were literally heaped. An unlucky terrorist whimpered, horribly maimed but somehow still alive.

This was, for sure, the real ideology of terror: violence and horrible death, not for any great and noble idea but for its own sake. This was their pulsing flow in excelsis.

In the far corner a half-dozen men had barricaded themselves behind an overturned table. One of them pointed at the man in black and shouted. Bolan emptied the rest of the M-16's magazine in their direction, heard shredded wood as the 5.56mm tumbler sought its fleshy target beyond the tabletop. By the time he heard the grunt of pain, he was prone on the floor and triggering the grenade launcher.

The HE round arced across the room and landed just in front of where the men were dug in. The blast sent bodies limp as rag dolls into the air, swallowing them with fire, rending them apart with shock waves.

Bolan snatched a full clip from a slit-pocket and rammed it home, then swept the room with the barrel of the gun. To his left a Japanese hardguy was leaning against the wall, his legs sticking out in front of him. Both hands were clasped over a hole in his stomach and gray brown entrails showed between his fingers. He stared at Bolan through unfocused eyes that reflected the sure awareness of imminent death. A mercy round between the eyes cured him of his leaking stomach.

Bolan moved back through the door and into the shadows. A few sporadic bursts of gunfire came from across the compound. Some of the terrorists had apparently made their way out.

The Executioner desired that a few of them survive. He wanted the word of what had happened in the Algerian desert to be known wherever and whenever the rest of this unholy brotherhood congregated. He wanted the enemy to realize that hellfire like this could rain down on any of them, anywhere, anytime; wanted that little nagging premonition of their own deaths to dog them every time they set out to wreak their havoc on others.

But there were four men not accounted for, and for them the terror trail had to end this night in this place.

18

Richard Wolfe knew.

In a crystal flash of clarity Wolfe understood that it had all been the work of that one man. Stone and Harker's "big bastard in black" and the guy who had taken out the radio and bushwacked the delegates were all one and the same. He must have hit that patrol outside the gates, before any of them had heard about the hit in Algiers. The son of a bitch had set out singlehandedly to tear apart everything that Harker and Wolfe had managed to put together over years.

And the guy had made it stick.

All this passed through Wolfe's mind in the messy second in which Luke Harker's head exploded off his shoulders.

Then he was moving automatically, leaping into operation with the fail-safe mechanism for survival that had brought him unscathed through a decade-plus of living on the violent edge.

He dropped to the floor and began crawling toward the door. The big guy in shades was already crashing through it. The air above Wolfe was alive with flying lead. Someone tripped over him and he saw a dark face in front of his, blood bubbling from the mouth but the eyes still animated with hate and hurt. A meaty hand closed around Wolfe's neck. He jammed the barrel of his .38 into the guy's supine torso and pulled the trigger. The noise of the small gun was swallowed by the louder bursts of automatic weapons elsewhere, but the hand fell away from his throat.

He felt a shock of impact in his left shoulder, like someone had punched him very, very hard with a closed fist, and he knew that a bullet had shattered the bone. He willed his body to keep moving, clawed at the floor with his right hand, dragged himself desperately forward, oblivious to anything but the gaping door now only a few feet away. Then he was outside, his face still pressed into the ground. But he was immobile.

He got the palm of his right hand flat against the dirt and managed to roll over. The pain it cost him wrenched a half-scream from his lips. He propped himself up in the shadows in time to see Frank Contadina stumble out of the door like he had been pushed. Then Jon Carter backed out. Somehow Carter had come up with a Kalashnikov, and he sent a rapid-fire spray of 7.62mm slugs into the meeting hall before turning and grabbing Contadina's arm.

'Carter,'' Wolfe called softly. "Help me.''

The other man turned and peered into the darkness.

"Over here," Wolfe said. "For God's sake help me."

Then the other man was standing over him. Wolfe blinked sweat out of his eyes.

The barrel of Carter's autorifle was six inches from his face. "You son of a bitch," Carter said tonelessly, and pulled the trigger.

The hammer clicked on an empty chamber.

"Carter," Contadina's crotchety voice snapped from somewhere behind them. "Get me out of here, goddammit."

Carter stared down at Wolfe, his face contorted with rage. He slammed the barrel of the AK-47 into the side of Wolfe's head, like he was taking a golf swing.

Wolfe rolled away from him, fiery needles of pain stabbing throughout his head and down into his shattered shoulder. A red film of his own blood obscured the sight of Carter grabbing Contadina roughly by the arm and jerking the older man toward the garage.

Wolfe wondered how far they'd get.

It didn't matter. None of it mattered now. He was going to die. He knew that now.

He was going to lie there and his blood was going to ooze out of his shoulder and disappear into the parched dirt until there wasn't any left, and Richard Wolfe of Flatbush was going to cash in his chips in the middle of the Sahara Desert several million miles from nowhere.

Like hell he was.

He got to his knees through sheer force of will. The rough pebbles cut into his legs and seemed to revive him enough to get him standing up. Nausea almost knocked him down again, but it passed. He wiped blood out of his eyes. He made one leg move in front of the other, did it again, lurched forward. One of the billets loomed up in front of him just as he reached the limit of his fading strength. He sat down clumsily, got his back against the building's wall, and hung his head between his knees.

Then the night flared into brilliant light. Not the bright clear light of daytime, but a hellish red glow that billowed up as if from the bowels of the earth.

Wolfe saw the top of the armory come off and the flames roll out in huge rolling balls.

Wolfe shook his head violently as waves of heat hit him. The movement tore a screaming protest of pain from his splintered shoulder, but it brought him back to his senses.

Scattered gunfire sounded around the compound. Someone hollered, "Charlie, is that you? It's Mick." The answer came in Arabic, punctuated by a shot. Apparently it hadn't been Charlie.

That's right, you assholes, shoot the hell out of each other. Think it through, Wolfe ordered himself. You sit here and get your strength back and then you get the hell out. Remember this: if you live, the bastard in black dies. You hire someone—some freelance ghoulish fucker like Rikki the Hyena—and he'll bring you Stone's head on a fucking platter.

Because that Stone guy wasn't human. That's how he could be in all those places at once. He was invulnerable and couldn't be killed. And that's not fair. You should be able to kill anyone.

Right then the big guy himself came out of the red shadows and stood looking around the compound like he owned the place. All right, Wolfe thought, so I'll kill the bastard myself. Except somewhere he'd lost the little .38.

That was okay. He was feeling stronger and he could take care of it any time. The guy in black wasn't there anymore, he'd just disappeared into thin air, and that was okay too.

Wolfe stood up and started between the billets toward the garage.

Something hit him from behind so hard he flew right off his feet. He plowed into the hard ground face first. He was beyond pain. By going beyond the parameters of life and health he had found the strength of the dead.

The first thing he realized was that there was no pain at all. Even his shoulder did not hurt anymore, and that was strange because he was lying on it. His mind was very clear and strangely bright.

The second thing he noticed was that he was unable to move his arms or legs.

The third thing was the pair of black sneakers in front of his face, and the two black legs going up from them.

Something flopped him over on his back.

The big man in the blacksuit looked down at him. His face was expressionless. There was ice in his eyes.

"Carter and Contadina," the guy said, his voice just as cold.

"I can't move."

"Where are they?"

Wolfe turned his eyes to one side and saw a guy crumpled on the ground a few yards away, a Kalashnikov still in his hands.

"Was he the one who got me?" Wolfe asked the big guy.

The icy one nodded.

Wolfe lightly laughed, a painful gurgle. The dead guy wore the TWPLF uniform. His name was Jake Something-or-other and a couple of nights ago Wolfe took him for sixty-five bucks in a poker game. There had to be something funny about that—buying the ranch from one of your own men. Didn't that take the fucking cake?

"Where are Carter and Contadina?" the man from blood said again. He had dropped to one knee and his face loomed over Wolfe. "You're dying, Wolfe."

"No pain," smiled the terrorist.

"Look." The guy propped up Wolfe's head, his touch surprisingly gentle. Wolfe looked down to where the man pointed.

There was a hole in the middle of his stomach. He could see shreds of his own gut hanging out of it.

"Your spinal cord is severed—that's why you can't feel anything. That's where the slug came out."

Blackness washed over Wolfe.

"It may take a couple of hours for you to bleed to death," the guy went on, insistent. "But you're dead."

Frigidity washed over him, seeped into every cell of his body, but the black shroud of cold fear was alive and it was eating him away, consuming him. The fear was utter and it was completely unbearable.

"Finish it," Wolfe whispered.

"Where are they?"

"Garage. . . saw them go toward the garage."

Time passed, and the acid terror-water ate at him, and he knew that in a moment his mind would collapse from the horror of it.

The hammer clicked back on a gun. Wolfe heard it from very far away, in the last vestigial reaches of his sanity.

It was the last sound he would ever hear in this place.

Bolan resheathed the AutoMag and moved off across the compound. Scattered fire continued to sound from various quarters.

Half-crouched, the blitzer dogtrotted down the row between the billets. Two men were covered in dancing flame, screaming. He kept in the shadows, stopping twice to check his backtrack. Here and there bodies littered the rubble.

Incredibly, less than fifteen minutes had passed since "Stone" walked into the jammed meeting hall.

Around him most of Luke Harker's compound had been reduced to charred remains of burned buildings, gnarled lengths of tangled chain-link, and jagged hunks of scrap metal as big as cars.

Bolan rechecked the luminous dial of his watch. He had fewer than ten minutes before Tex and the girl were to take off, and he planned to make that meet. The girl was the original mission. Bolan would not consider the mission complete until he saw to his own satisfaction that she was safely away from this hellhole.

As it was, he had taken an unusual chance in making the field decision to take on Harker and his convocation of terror. He had not been in touch with Stony Man Farm at any time. But it was a necessary risk. He would always act independently of Hal Brognola when the circumstances demanded it. Although Hal would hate to hear that. In very many ways Hal was a big man too, and he had big feelings. He worried too much.

So far, Bolan's decision had proved to be the correct one.

So far.

The job was not yet over. Bolan knew the mission *could* not be complete until he had taken care of Frank Contadina. And his sidekick, Jon Carter the Black Ace.

Bolan's decimation of Harker's terrorist summit would leave a temporary vacuum in the netherworld of international political violence. And Capo Frank

Contadina was bound to abhor that vacuum and be only too happy to fill it from his own ranks.

Contadina had been building the bridges between organized crime and the international terrorist conspiracy for months, maybe years. It would be easy for him to complete the vows of that horrific matrimony. The result would be a new and even more powerful alliance.

Bolan had to stop it now.

He came around the smoldering remnants of the last billet in the row, and one-half of his quest came to an end.

Frank Contadina was lying on his back in the rubble. His shiny summer suit was torn and his face was smeared with blood and dirt. The new international top *capo* no longer looked like a businessman, a rakish sportsman, or a shrewd survivor of the king-of-the-hill battle for criminal supremacy.

He looked like a dying old man.

Blood welled from a sucking wound in the left side of his chest. He was still breathing, but had to gasp for air to fill his punctured lung. He looked up at the man in black and a measure of recognition came into his dying eyes. He muttered something.

Bolan bent in time to hear the single word: "Carter."

Yeah, that figured. The Black Ace had decided his boss was suddenly a liability in the battle for survival, and he had taken the simple expedient of unloading the burden. "Loyalty" lost most of its meaning when a lousy guy's back was against the wall—as Frank Contadina had just learned.

Twenty meters of open space separated Bolan from the garage. A jeep was parked in front of its open door.

There was a machine gun tripod-mounted on the open back platform of the rig. In the flickering firelight cast by the nearby burning billets, Bolan could see Jon Carter crouched behind the rig, using it to shield his body, his hands gripping the big gun's twin handles.

"Drop it," Carter shouted.

Bolan did not move. He was still hurting from the side wound. But his mind was nicely focused.

"It's over, Stone," Carter called. His voice sounded charged with triumph. "Drop it or I drop you."

Bolan let the M-203 fall to the dirt.

Carter grinned, his face shiny in the flame light.

"One of us is getting out of here alive," Carter yelled. "It's not going to be you."

The guy was cool. Cool, yeah, but nervous. So he talked too much, it was that simple.

The nightfighter was already fingering the little black box in his chest pack.

Bolan gently pressed the third and fourth buttons on the detonator.

The top came off the garage, the flash preceding the *whump*, allowing Bolan the uncanny sight of silent disintegration.

Carter had time to open his mouth, but whatever

sound he would have made never came out as a howling tongue of flame flattened him, bursting forth from the compound's fuel storage tank. The image stayed in Bolan's retina of a man screaming fire instead of words, as if Jon Carter's mouth was spewing flames from a force that was coming through the back of his head. Now the high-up hood lay invisible beneath the fireball, incinerating to dust.

Carter's boss still lay at Bolan's feet. Contadina was staring up at him.

There was a rattling sound deep in the old man's chest and then a globule of blood, bright red in the unnatural light of the gasoline-fed flames, slobbered out of his mouth and the wide eyes went dead.

Bolan shouldered the weapon and turned his back on the hellgrounds for good.

19

Another green Land Rover from the late Harker's nationwide fleet of jeeps was parked at the compound gate. Bolan got behind the wheel and tromped down on the starter. Bent low in the seat he piloted it through the shattered gates and started back to where he had left Tex Hoffman and Jill Breton.

A single pistol shot cracked somewhere behind him, but he was already out of handgun range.

Once he reached the foot of the bluff he let the rig coast to a stop and sat still, both hands on the steering wheel. The wound in his side throbbed, an aching reminder of the hellfire he had left behind.

No, he had not left it behind him. Mack Bolan knew there would be more of the same ahead. Other fights in the One Big and True Fight to keep the world out of the hands of those who made it a place where the man with the gun intimidates everyone else.

And yeah, Mack Bolan was tired.

He had not slept for two days and during that time he had been going at a pace that would have stopped others cold. It would be another half-day before he could get Jill Breton to anyplace with communication to the outside world. He would make it, sure, but he was already running on auxiliary reserves of both physical and mental energy.

Yet his combat sense remained on full alert. And suddenly it was signaling trouble.

He approached his own basecamp with lights out, bringing his Rover to a stop fifty meters from where the other Rover sat. He could see it clearly in the bright desert starlight.

But no people.

He took the M-203 and went EVA, all fatigue forgotten, every nerve once again sensitized to danger.

Tex Hoffman was sitting behind the wheel of the Rover, slumped a little in the seat. Bolan pulled open the rig's door.

Tex tumbled out at his feet and his Stetson rolled off to one side.

There was a neat entry wound in the middle of his forehead. The blood was still shiny wet. There was no sign of the girl.

Bolan pulled the dead man out of the Rover and climbed in himself. All his gear was stashed in the back, so this was the vehicle he would now use. With these wheels he would hunt down the recaptured girl to keep her in her newfound faith and, too, to avenge the word of honor that Tex Hoffman had kept but which had been betrayed by stinking reality. He found and seized the infrared nightscope, cursing the seconds he had lost in reverie as he had approached the violated camp.

The top of the bluff was the highest point for many miles. Standing on the hood of the screenless Rover, he commanded a powerful view down the five-thousand-dollar electron tube whose mercury battery allowed him to cut through the night. He started his scan to the north, the most likely direction for anyone but a lunatic to take.

And saw a jeep about a half mile off, heading up the faint trail he himself had come down less than a day before. It was putting territory behind it fast.

Bolan hit the starter, slammed the floor-shift forward, wrenched at the wheel. He jounced and bucked through the cut of the ancient streambed, the two rear wheels leaving the ground, then he was tearing down off the bluff.

He hit the flat sand of the desert at fifty miles per hour and accelerating. His trajectory cut across a curve in the trail and allowed for a beeline on the lead vehicle. His foot was flat to the floor-metal. The low-geared engine whined in its extremity.

The driver of the other jeep did not expect pursuit, let alone by a superior vehicle. He had not expected to be hunted down by the Rolls-Royce of modern field vehicles. His own jeep, a Willys, was tough, even fast, but it was not strong—strong in the sense of enduring and unstoppable. Every rock his front wheels hit was to his disadvantage, to the Land Rover's advantage. The Rover ate up obstacles and ejected them like a boost.

Bolan closed to within two hundred meters when

the other guy risked a quick glance over his shoulder.

The starlight illuminated the round face of Rikki the Hyena.

The little psychopath mercenary had figured out the key to his continued advancement through the ranks of international terrorism: the Project Little Bang prototype bomb.

And the key to that piece of hardware was Jill Breton.

The jeep's engine rose in pitch, but Bolan matched its speed. He saw Jill's blond head start to turn to look back at him but Rikki's hand darted out, the closed fist smashing her in the face. The rig veered violently and Bolan picked up several yards.

Bolan had one advantage. As the pursuer he could keep an eye on the man ahead of him, while Rikki had to trust to instinct.

But he suffered an equal disadvantage. He had to keep Jill Breton from harm at all costs.

Rikki would have no such compunction.

The enraged Jill Breton chose that moment to lurch across the seat at the terrorist. The lead jeep swerved wildly. For a moment the two right wheels lifted, then slammed back as the vehicle skewed with the renewed traction.

Bolan saw the flash of the gun in Rikki's hand. He slashed at the girl and she slumped away.

Now Bolan was less than fifty yards behind and closing.

Rikki swung around, steering blindly with his left hand, a Skorpion machine pistol in his right. Fire flashed from the muzzle.

A spray of 7.65mm tumblers tattooed a ragged line across the desert floor in front of him. Bolan held the wheel steady, his foot still flat on the floor.

But he was doing something in addition. Bolan was grasping the big Weatherby Mark V and cradling it in his right arm.

It was an improbable shot. Improbable, yeah, but not impossible. Bolan had scored six-inch groupings with the rifle at 400 meters.

Of course, that was from a prone position on a firing range. The gun was so powerful, the way he was holding it now it was like a monster. He would have to close the distance at least another ten yards to have any chance at all.

But it was the only chance he would get.

He rested the rifle along the line of the hood. The stock was nestled hard against his shoulder.

The rear bumper of the lead jeep was twenty yards in front.

Bolan clutched the steering wheel between his knees. There was no time to sight. His years of experience with the big gun, his innate sense of aim, those would have to serve.

The heavy recoil slammed the butt into Bolan's shoulder. The split-second flash illuminated the night. The jeep ahead of him continued to barrel forward.

Then, imperceptibly at first and then more quickly, it began to slow.

Bolan pulled the Rover to a juddering stop. Ahead of him Rikki's jeep lurched twice and stalled.

Bolan came up on foot, the AutoMag ready in his hand.

Rikki was slumped forward over the wheel. What had been his plump round face was now a mask of red. No features were visible. His brains were splattered across the dashboard.

Jill Breton moaned and stirred. Bolan came around to her side of the jeep. He took her under her arms and pulled her out. There was a fresh bruise, livid, high on one side of the girl's forehead but when her eyes fluttered open they were clear and focused.

Before Bolan could stop her she twisted around and looked at what was left of Rikki the Hyena.

She started to scream. Bolan let her. If she got it out now, maybe it would not come back during those long nights of memory that was now her legacy of terror.

The screams turned to groans, and she came into his arms. The hard man held her with infinite gentleness. He could feel the warm tears soaking through the material of the blacksuit.

She stopped crying finally. "I'm...I'm sorry," she breathed. "It's over now," she said.

"I wish," murmured Bolan. His ears, despite the droning of the Rover that had deafened him, picked up bad news.

"You drive," he barked at the girl. She leaped for the driver's seat. She had heard it too.

The whine of another jeep.

Some of Harker's damned goons were in chase after Rikki. Now as headless as Rikki himself, the TWPLF organization was each man for himself. And some of them wanted what Rikki had tried to get.

The sound came reverberating from the south. Jill pressed the Rover into life and withdrew the clutch fast. The vehicle hurled itself forward and she grappled with the wheel to keep the thing straight and on track.

In the passenger seat, Bolan looked behind them. He was sitting sideways to his driver. He started to handle the gleaming AutoMag. He was going to shoot for the eyes or the heart. No more grandstanding with an aristocrat's gun in a bucking 4WD.

So Tex had not been so honorable after all. The slippery bastard had informed on their position, probably directly to the late ungreat Ricardo while Bolan was pulling the girl out of the compound and Tex was supposed to be on patrol. Somehow he had gotten word through, to the one man he thought was as disconnected as himself. And that had backfired right into his forehead.

Not so much slippery as just plain scared. With a little bit of clever. And now a hole in his brain. Ah, well.

The creeps coming at Bolan at this moment were

nameless assholes who were after the Hyena only because they knew where he was.

Yeah, that would be some foul fate, to be finished by a bunch of unhinged soldierboys who were chasing anything that moved.

No way would it go down like that. Bolan had a spunky ward to protect, the girl at the wheel who was going through the gears like some speed-crazed trucker.

He smiled as he rose to scan their rear, anchoring himself by pressing his knees against seat and dash. Stones flew up at him from the wildly spinning wheels.

"Got anything to protect your eyes?" he yelled down at her. Without looking away from the desert-scape, she reached under the dash with her left hand and pulled out Stone's own aviators.

"These'll do," she called, determined as any driver in all history to eat up the desert, every inch of it to the coast. If she was unfamiliar with a right-hand-drive British vehicle, she still knew where the shades would be stashed.

In the left-hand passenger space, Bolan continued his observations, brazenly standing like a target.

He did not like to be chased. A warrior chases. He would work on that angle right now.

A flash cut the air. AK-47 fire. Straight at them from their now visible pursuers.

The jeep didn't have a chance against the Rover, but Bolan wanted rid of them anyway. Jill ducked down and continued aiming the Rover straight ahead.

"Start turning to the right in a giant loop," called Bolan. "Can you hear? Make it a wide turn, nothing sharp."

So this kill was going to be up to her . . . it would be a reward for her decision to go straight. Maybe a fast, sharp kill that she was truly a part of might wipe out the horrors that would otherwise torment her.

"We'll lead them astray and then we'll finish them off," laughed the Executioner, loud in the night for her to hear him, loud against the blankness of this stony desert to recharge his energies and be done with the dead place once and for all. Led astray, then damn near done in. That was her story all right. But this time it was *she* who was in charge.

The turn had quietened the automatic fire. Lost in the night, the vehicles were cat and mouse with claws retracted, teeth hidden, while a fix on their positions became the method of the game.

"Where are they?" shouted the girl, leaning slightly out of the right side as she held tightly to the vibrating wheel. "Do you see them?"

Bolan made no reply. Instead he knelt down and planted his big hand on the parking-brake that jutted from the floor between the two seats.

He yanked it up with all his might.

The proud vehicle slammed to a halt like it had been hit in the nose.

"Keep it running! Keep it running!" yelled Jill's

giant mentor. Her foot was pushing the clutch damn near through the floor as the engine raced, clear of the gears. The deceleration from flat out to zero had put her face inches over the top of the steering wheel and her foot deep into the floor without any trouble at all.

Bolan released the taut hand brake.

"Now back up!" he shouted.

The impact of the stop had sent his hunched shoulder banging into the dash panel. Now the acceleration in reverse jerked him once more against the panel. His wound screamed. It was in the lap of the gods whether real damage would be done there. A thought raced through his mind as the Rover under the young girl's control tore backward to its fate. "I'm human. I'm only human," said that mind.

But as he stood again, once more bracing his legs for support, Bolan acted as if he were immortal.

The pursuing jeep was fifty yards behind them and the gap closed like elevator doors. The chatter of a Russian automatic started up and the Executioner took a bead on its source.

Now Bolan was the cat.

The AutoMag spat. And spat. And spat.

The enemy jeep was already wobbling in confusion as the driver took time to figure out the bizarre approach of the Rover. But the driver was already dead as he went through that exercise. What began as a dither of perplexity became an outright slide into chaos. The jeep slewed to one side with its steering wheel covered in the gray gore that splashed onto it, sparkling in the starlight as minuscule windshield shards stuck to the organic matter.

There were two other men in the jeep. Or once there were. They were no longer men. The slugs had torn through their tensed bodies and released their nervous systems into spastic activity, their now-meaningless musculature whipping itself into epilepsy as the sudden new holes in their bodies gushed blood over each other's flapping forms. Fare thee well, dumb assholes.

Jill braked the Rover. She turned for the first time since roaring into reverse. She saw the jeep behind them roll away to her right, three slumped forms still jerking in it as it lost control over the rocky terrain and stalled to halt in no direction that mattered.

"Those are yours," Bolan said quietly, standing above her, his legs apart in the passenger well, the AutoMag at rest, his jaw grim as he looked out into the gloom at the gun's fine handiwork. "You made them a target. You did well. They're not a target anymore."

Jill Breton shuddered.

For her it was truly over.

For Bolan it would never be over.

A twist of hot pain shot through his side. So his opened flesh would have to heal in the continuing battle, not in any nonexistent peace. He had been hurt in his last warring visit to Algeria, and it had presaged no surcease in his crusade back then.

Same now. There was never any time to be wounded.

"Jill, your father is waiting for you," grunted Bolan. "Let's go home."

Jill pulled herself up from her seat and snaked her arms around him. They stood there in exhausted embrace, a silhouette of life, of upright quiet endurance, amidst the emptiness of the desert.

It was dawn by the time they released each other.

About the author

The story of Don Pendleton's success reads much like the fiction he has created. A native of Arkansas, Pendleton left home at fourteen to join the navy. "I didn't falsify any documents, I simply told the recruiters I was 18 and they signed me up." He saw action in World War II—in the North Atlantic, North Africa, Iwo Jima and Okinawa—and, later, in Korea. After war service, he completed his high-school equivalency and worked as a railroad telegrapher, air-traffic controller and as an executive in the aerospace industry.

Married and the father of six, Pendleton describes himself as a self-taught writer who is "simply a storyteller, an entertainer who hopes to enthrall with visions of the reader's own innate greatness."

The exploits of his hero, Mack Bolan, have sold more than 30 million copies in North America and 65 million worldwide, having been translated into 12 languages and sold in 125 countries.

Don Pendleton's

MACK
BOLAN

THE EXECUTIONER SERIES

Most people have no conception of the extent of the terrorist threat, because they do not think they are touched by it. They are wrong. The very existence of so-called humans who see their fellow humans as inanimate things to be abused at will, diminishes every person who permits such a thing to go on.

> —Mack Bolan, a.k.a. Col. John Phoenix,
> THE EXECUTIONER

Mack Bolan is back, with a story every month to record his incredible career, the third mile in a life devoted to avenging wrong and—by fierce strength and selfless love—maintaining the qualities we know as civilization.

Now operating behind the identity of Col. John Phoenix, Mack Bolan is still, as he will forever be, his own man. Stony Man Farm may be government-owned, but Stony Man is really his, and the entire

Stony Man operation falls under Bolan's direct management in total autonomy.

Mack, once "Sergeant USA," known to the entire world as "The Executioner," is conducting a war easily the equal of the earlier furious one fought in the longest and bloodiest campaign against organized crime the world had ever seen. It is a new war against grave threats to national security and, uniquely, it has the covert sponsorship of the U.S. government.

The true gravity of this war is underscored by the number of Mafia characters and others of the vilest criminality that Bolan finds slinking around behind the new enemy lines. The Executioner has always figured that the roll call of terrorism is a roll call of endless shame. His enemies are not political, nor are they religious: they are simply indefensible.

But there is an honor roll in the new war—the names of those whom Bolan has sought to save and the names of those who have helped him in those bloody battles of salvation in his six most recent missions:

Laconia, a brave agent mercilessly tortured to the very edge of what any man could bear....

Soraya, the fine Arab woman who helped Bolan face the hell on earth that was Colombia in hurricane season....

Adamian and Hagen, two men of noble ancestry who came their own separate ways to the same hangman's trapdoor....

Kabrina, the 25-year-old Turkish beauty who shared death-defying danger with Bolan, to earn heroic integrity and a high place in the life of her free country....

Hook, the devoted soldier who sacrificed his life for Bolan....

Fran Traynor, policewoman without compare whose independence routed Bolan directly to the viral source of a bad outbreak of midwestern corruption....

Carol Nazarour, brave American woman who threw in her lot with Bolan and lived to rejoice that she had....

The men and women of the Meo Hmong in Vietnam who, with Mack Bolan's example to guide them, brought grace and magnificence to the centuries-old tradition of South Vietnamese loyalty....

Jill Breton, the wayward girl who became all woman when Bolan showed her that a trigger is for taking a shot, fast, without doubts or uncertainties; just do what has to be done and done immediately....

These have been great people in magnificent adventures and they shine brightly in the reflection of the life-affirming power that will always radiate from the soldier of violent rebirth: Mack Bolan.

It has been a long and bloody road since Hal Brognola first offered Bolan a new kind of life in "Sensitive Operations."

"I couldn't sit at a desk, Hal," Bolan had countered when Hal first suggested the new job.

"You won't *have* a desk, buddy," Brognola replied with a laugh.

"I'd have to pick my own key people."

"Naturally."

And pick them Mack did, with a vengeance: Jack Grimaldi, the flyboy still crazy with life; Pol Blancanales, now fighting with Stony Man's new Able Team; Leo Turrin; Konzaki, the armorer; April Rose, the lovely, lively April; and for overseas, the incredible Phoenix Force.

"And you're going to find echoes of the Mob in everything you touch. It's the same war, the same kind of enemy. You haven't been fighting *people*— you've been fighting a *condition*."

A hell of an interesting offer from Hal, and now the logic of it was unfolding in the Executioner's third mile.

Every mission thus far had been timely to within a radar blip of the front pages of the world's newspapers. South American bloodshed in *The New War*; Turkish-American terrorism in *Double Crossfire*, a story published simultaneously with the deaths in American streets of two senior Turkish diplomats; a psychopathic killer protected by an abuse of justice in *The Violent Streets*; the reality of a foreign-paid hit team operating within shooting distance of Washington, D.C., in *The Iranian Hit*; the continuing heart-rending tragedy of abandoned POWs in Southeast Asia in *Return to Vietnam*; the historical propensity for evil to link up into huge international congresses and then to fall apart in paranoia and acrimony in *Terrorist Summit*.

Mack Bolan is a Winner!

**Millions of fans from all walks of life applaud
The Executioner, a warrior who affirms the sanctity of life**

"I am a specialist, fourth class in the U.S. Army. I am a very devoted Mack Bolan fan, as are many GIs. He is the man we all wish we were and try to be. I hope you keep the series coming for years and years!"

H.B.W., APO, New York

"Mack Bolan has changed my life. I went from a housewife whose major interest was the price of groceries to an alert and interested citizen who reads the paper avidly and knows how to vote intelligently."

C.T., Prior, Oklahoma

"As a college English major, I consider myself fortunate to possess the entire Executioner series. For guts, determination, dedication and all-out American-style hell-bent-for-leather warfare, the wildass warrior takes a back seat to no one!"

C.R.E., Marquette, Michigan

"I am a Vietnam vet and I find your stories very accurate. You researched them well. I look forward to each book."

D.L., Vancouver, Washington

"I am in junior high school and I enjoy reading your books very much because they are adventurous and about real life."

S.B., Iowa

"I am thirty-nine, a housewife and college educated. I am hooked on Mack. I hungrily await the next book."

B.H., Denton, Texas

"I'm seventeen years old and a Bolan fanatic. Seventeen is a time of self-doubt, a traumatic time, but I've found someone I can relate to and that person is Mack Bolan. He is so real and so caring."

B.W., Long Beach, California

"Mack Bolan is the best anti-terrorist fighter we have. May the world of The Executioner go on forever."

J.D.K.,* Toronto, Ontario

"I am ecstatic over the return of The Executioner. It's been so long since we Bolan fans have heard the ring of the marksman's medal."

D.S., Defiance, Ohio

"I was offered $1,000 for my complete mint collection of Executioner first editions, and I turned it down. I hope that tells you what I feel about Mack Bolan."

S.M., Zanesville, Ohio

"I was first introduced to The Executioner by my boyfriend, who must be one of Mack Bolan's biggest fans (and so am I now!). The series is a breakthrough."

T.K.S., Rolla, Michigan

"I cannot thank you enough for the thrill and excitement the Executioner has brought me. My life has been enriched!"

D.O., Jacksonville, Florida

"For my money, the Executioners are the best books out, with the best stories."

R.G., Champaign, Illinois

*Names available on request.

Mack Bolan, captain of his own fate, protector of his own identity — Gold Eagle's hero blazes his way to success!

"The greatest book series on the market."

J.R.,* Angola, Louisiana

"I am in the air force, and if I ever have to fight, I know I will feel as Mack Bolan does. I will not be fighting men, but fighting for ideals."

K.W.F., Kingston, Tennessee

"For two years I was constantly truant from school. Then I read The Executioner series and grasped the meaning of Bolan's philosophy of living large. Now I take school as the challenge it is."

R.M., San Francisco, California

"Mack Bolan is a symbol to all of us who, if we were but half the man Mack is, would be out there waging our war against crime."

S.E.G., Baltimore, Maryland

"My greatest respect — you're tops!"

P.C., Arnold, Missouri

"I am twenty-one and in the navy. When I stumbled onto Mack Bolan, my first reaction was WOW! I just can't get over the realism."

B.S., U.S.S. James Monroe

"I am impatiently awaiting the next chapter in The Executioner saga. Can you hurry it up a bit? *Please?*"

K.H., Forest City, North Carolina

*Names available on request.